Brampton Publishers Ltd,
The Gate, Keppoch Street,
Cardiff CF24 3JW

Text copyright © C.C. Brampton 2022
Cover illustrations © C.C. Brampton 2022

First published in 2022 by Brampton Publishers Ltd

www.ccbrampton.com

eBook ISBN: 978-0-9935568-4-5
Paperback ISBN: 978-0-9935568-5-2

Print and bound by affiliates of Amazon KDP Publishing.

C.C. BRAMPTON

Brampton Publishers Ltd

DEDICATION

For my wife Sarah who has shown me love and
support throughout my writing madness,
I intend to prove them all wrong!

And for my three darling cherry winkles,
Ira-leigh, Ava and Shia I love you to the moon and back!

Don't follow the trend, be the trend.

CONTENTS

CHAPTER 1

A NOISE IN THE SKY

I t was a warm, sunny Saturday in the town of Cravins Creek. Charles Theodore Sprewell, known to his friends as Charlie, and his beloved dog, Skyla, was going with his two best friends, Bridget and Whizzy, to play in the forest nearby. The children loved nothing more than spending time together running about the forest that surrounded their small town.

Cravins Creek Forest was home to some of the tallest trees in California. It was an enchanting forest teeming with beautiful flowers and delicious fruits, such as blackberries and blue elderberry. There were endless secret paths and trails to explore and, further up the creek, there were magnificent waterfalls and glistening rock pools to swim in. Wild animals – elk, mountain lions and black bears – also lived in the forest, and the children came across them every now and then. This never deterred the children from going there, for they knew to keep well away.

Anyone wandering through the forest would hear the children laughing as they played. But on that warm, sunny Saturday there was an abrupt, dreadful screaming noise. It came from high above their heads. The children stopped and stared around in bewilderment. Moments later, there was an almighty bang that shook the forest.

'What was that?' shrieked Bridget, hiding behind Whizzy, who was hiding behind Charlie.

Out of the three children, Charlie was considered the strongest and bravest. He relished in adventure, solving mysteries and doing daring stuff. He also had a penchant for mischief and a reputation for being a hothead. At eleven, he was the oldest of the three by a few months. He was slightly taller than Bridget and Whizzy and had an athletic build, dishevelled blond hair and green eyes. But what set Charlie apart from his best friends was his sporting talent: he was one heck of a baseball hitter.

Baseball was Charlie's life. When he wasn't mucking around with his friends, he'd be out in his back yard, practising. It was his dream to become a professional baseball player one day and do his late father proud. Sadly, his dad had died, serving his country, when Charlie was nine. Unlike Bridget and Whizzy, who had older sisters, Charlie was an only child, and he lived at home with his mom, Debby, and her partner.

The second oldest of the three friends was Cody Carter, or Whizzy, as his friends called him. He was a wizard at using computers and loved inventing things, hence his nickname. Whizzy was fascinated by space gadgets and anything technological. His greatest wish had always been to meet an alien. He was a slight African American, and he wore round, thick-framed glasses. Without them, he was as blind as a bat.

Lastly, there was Bridget Ann Gunnarsson, the youngest of the three – and the most cautious. Bridget had glowing autumn-brown hair that matched her eyes. She loved horses. Her mom was British and her dad was American. The family were not short of a penny or two. For five generations they had owned a large manufacturing business in Cravins Creek called Gunnarsson Timber.

The three best friends were inseparable.

'It sounded like a plane!' Charlie said, staring up at the sliver of blue sky between the treetops.

'It sounded more like the forest broke in half, if you ask me,' Whizzy said, looking around.

'Perhaps it was the Red Lady coming to claim her revenge,' Bridget commented.

'Shuddup, Bridget, everyone knows that's just a stupid made-up story to scare kids into going to bed.' Charlie shook his head.

'Well, I think it's true,' Bridget argued.

'You would,' said Charlie.

'Whatever it was, it didn't sound good, that's for sure,' said Whizzy.

'You can say that again. Even Skyla's freaked out – easy, girl.' Charlie tried to calm her.

Charlie's dog was an old black and white border collie with mismatched eyes: one was brown, the other sky blue. Charlie's father had wanted to name her Chewy, since she chewed almost everything in sight – but Charlie believed the real reason was his father's adoration of *Star Wars* and Chewbacca. However, Charlie firmly insisted on the dog being called Skyla.

'It's getting late. Maybe we should consider heading back, you guys,' Bridget suggested.

Charlie gave a cheeky grin. 'Or maybe we should go check out that noise, see where it came from,' he said.

Skyla suddenly shot off between the trees.

'Oh no, Charlie!' Bridget cried. 'Skyla's taken off!'

Charlie called for Skyla to return, but she didn't. He started to panic. It was not like Skyla to run off; she was a very loyal dog and stuck by Charlie's side everywhere he went. Skyla was the fourth member of the children's gang, and her unexpectedly darting off worried the children.

'Quick, help me find her, you guys!' Charlie said, urgency in his voice.

The children sprinted through the forest, calling out to her, but there was no response. Finally, they stopped to catch their breath.

'Any sign of her, Charlie?' Whizzy said, pushing his glasses back up his nose.

Charlie grunted. 'I don't know what's got into her!'

'Perhaps we should report her to the forest rangers,' Bridget suggested.

'No!' Charlie replied bluntly. 'We don't have time. We need to keep looking for her. It'll be quicker if we split up – you two go that way and I'll—'

'Wait a minute! Did you hear that?' Bridget said, looking around. 'It sounds like barking.'

Charlie cocked his head. 'It sounds like Skyla, but where is she? I can't see her!'

'Ooh – it sounded as if it came from over there!' Whizzy said, pointing in the direction of a gnarled oak tree.

'C'mon, you guys!' Charlie said, beckoning the other two. He sprinted through the undergrowth while the other two did their best to keep up with him. They ran down a dip and up the other side, through a gap between the trees. There, by the edge of a small cliff, was Skyla, barking. Charlie called to her, and she ran back to him.

'There you are!' Charlie cried out with relief, kneeling to give her a big hug. Whizzy and Bridget followed with flushed faces and out of breath.

'Thank goodness we found her,' said Bridget.

'What in the blazes has got into you, girl?' Charlie said, grabbing Skyla's furry face.

While Charlie and Bridget were making a fuss of her, Whizzy walked over to the cliff edge and cautiously peered over. His eyes widened.

'Hey, you guys, come take a look at this!' he called.

Charlie and Bridget joined him and glanced over. At the bottom of the cliff, in a grassy clearing, lay a plane. It had broken into pieces that were strewn across the grass.

'It looks like we've found what made that noise,' Whizzy said, raising his eyebrows.

'See, what did I tell you? I told you it was a plane!' said Charlie excitedly. 'And they say that nothing ever happens out in the Tules. Huh.'

'Holy cow!' Bridget said, taken aback. 'Do you think anyone's down there?'

'Difficult to say from up here,' said Whizzy.

'Well, there's only one way to find out. We need to go down there and check it out!' said Charlie, turning to head off.

'Oh no!' Bridget said, crossing her arms.

Charlie stopped in his tracks. 'Why not?'

'Because who wants to see some dead body? I for sure don't. You just want to go down there so you can snoop about,' said Bridget.

'That's not true!' said Charlie defensively.

'Really?' said Bridget, raising an eyebrow.

'There could be someone hurt down there who needs our help!' Charlie pointed out.

'In that case, we should tell the forest rangers,' Bridget said.

Charlie shook his head. 'By the time we go and find them, someone in that plane could've died. Can you live with that on your conscience?'

'Oh, don't you go playing the guilt trick on me, Charlie Sprewell!' Bridget said crossly, wagging her finger at him.

'Alright, you guys!' Whizzy said, stepping between them. 'Let's take a step back and calm down.'

They glared at one another, then Charlie deliberately turned his back and whispered to Whizzy, 'What do you say, Whizzy? Wanna go down there and check it out?' He jerked his head towards the cliff edge.

Whizzy looked apprehensive. He scratched his head. 'Er...'

'Argh, c'mon, you guys,' Charlie said, huffing and puffing and flapping his arms about the place like an angry cockerel, 'where's your sense of adventure?'

'Well, since you asked, it's back home watching *Bonnie and the Dream Team* while eating double chocolate chip ice cream. Mmm, sweet heaven!' Bridget said.

'That's such a stupid TV show,' Charlie retorted.

'Well, I like it,' Bridget said. 'I wouldn't expect your pea-size brain to understand.'

'Look, we're wasting time here squabbling. There's only one way to resolve this. I'm calling a vote,' Charlie declared.

'Not again, Charlie,' Bridget grumbled. 'That'll be the second time this week – do we really have to?'

Bridget was not fond of Charlie calling pack votes because she always lost. The deciding vote always seemed to fall on Whizzy, who usually sided with Charlie.

'Yes, we do,' Charlie said firmly. 'You know the rule: if we all can't agree on something, we call it. Say the words, you guys.'

Bridget rolled her eyes.

'The blood of my pack is stronger than ever, only if the three of us stick together,' they said in unison, then they gave each other their secret handshake.

'Alright, now that's out of the way, let's vote!' Charlie said, rubbing his hands together. 'Raise your hand if you *don't* want to go down there and check it out.'

Bridget was the only one to raise her arm, which came as no surprise to her.

'That's one to you, Bridget,' Charlie said smugly. 'Now, raise your hand if you *do* want to go down there and check it out.'

Charlie couldn't raise his arm fast enough or high enough. But he was the only one who did. He looked at Whizzy, who was staring at the ground.

'Er, Whizzy, what are you doing? Why haven't you raised your hand?' Charlie enquired.

'I'm undecided,' Whizzy said, folding his arms.

'What?' Charlie said indignantly. 'What do you mean, you're undecided?' Knitting his brow with annoyance, he walked up to Whizzy and got in his face. 'Whizzy, you know you have to vote! How else are we going to decide what we're doing?'

Whizzy looked across at Bridget, as if to say 'what do I do?' But Bridget just shrugged. Whizzy turned timid the moment his eyes reconnected with Charlie's.

'Fine, let's go check it out,' Whizzy said, reluctantly raising his hand.

'Awesome! That's two votes in favour to go!' Charlie said, elated. 'Sorry Bridget, but you lose.'

'Gee, Charlie, I would never have guessed,' Bridget said sarcastically, glaring at Whizzy as she brushed past him.

'What's up with her?' Charlie said, turning to Whizzy with a perplexed expression. 'It was a fair vote.'

Whizzy shook his head and patted Charlie on the shoulder. 'Forget it, Charlie. C'mon.' The boys set off after her.

CHAPTER 2

THE MEN IN MASKS

The children soon forgot their difference of opinion. They picked their way carefully down the narrow mossy trail that led to the foot of the cliff. The trail wound among the giant redwoods.

As always, Charlie led the way, with Skyla trotting along soberly behind him. He was desperate to see the downed plane. If he could have waved a magic wand and made himself disappear then reappear at the plane, he would have.

It was some time before they reached the bottom. There, the land flattened out and the trail snaked off between tall green spruces. They crossed the creek and were soon at the edge of the clearing where the plane lay.

They hesitated.

'There it is,' said Charlie excitedly.

'You know, I'm getting a bad feeling about this,' said Bridget.

'You get a bad feeling about everything we do, Bridget!' Charlie said. 'Quit complaining, would you?'

'Well, sorry, but we can't all be as brave as you! Ain't that right, Whizzy?' Bridget turned to him.

Whizzy looked caught by the question. 'Huh? I'm brave!' he said, standing up straight and squaring his shoulders.

'Yeah, right, and I'm Wonder Woman.' Bridget snorted. 'Whizzy, you still sleep with your bedroom light on, so I believe that counts you out.'

'Well, at least I'm not scared of the Red Lady, unlike some!' Whizzy argued.

'You wouldn't be saying that if she was here right now and came after you!' Bridget snapped.

'Quit it!' Charlie spat. He looked all around to see if the disturbance had drawn the attention of anyone else. But other than the sound of the creek and the chirping of birds, it was quiet.

'C'mon, let's check it out.'

The trio jogged across the field, Skyla running beside Charlie. Before long they found themselves wandering warily amid the scattered debris of the broken plane. The nose of the plane was nowhere in sight. However, the middle section through to the tail lay buried in the earth. One of the wings had broken off and there was a large hole in its side. The children stood before the ghastly sight, shocked.

Bridget held her hand to her mouth. 'Good lord!'

Charlie looked at Bridget, frowning. Hesitantly he walked towards the plane.

'What are you doing?' asked Bridget.

'I want to see if there's anyone's inside,' replied Charlie.

Bridget and Whizzy stood watching with anxious expressions as Charlie climbed carefully onto the twisted, jagged metal. He poked his head into the large hole.

'Jeepers!' he said in a surprised voice.

'What is it? Please tell me it's not a dead body you've found, Charlie! I can't bear to see,' Bridget said, turning away to bury her face in Whizzy's shoulder.

'The opposite. It's empty,' he said.

'Thank goodness,' Bridget said, placing her hand on her chest.

'Empty?' Whizzy said, wrinkling his forehead.

'Yep.' Charlie turned to them. 'Come see for yourself.'

'I'll take your word for it,' said Bridget.

'I will!' said Whizzy brightly. Charlie climbed down and Whizzy climbed up to take a look.

'He's right, there's nothing in here,' Whizzy said. 'It looks like it could be a transport plane – there are no seats.'

'So what made it crash?' said Bridget.

'Who knows?' Charlie shrugged. 'Planes fall out the sky for all sorts of reasons.'

Charlie glanced over to see where Skyla had gone and caught sight of her disappear round the back of the plane. He followed her, ducking under the wing, to find her clawing at something. It looked like a dented chrome box.

'Hey, what is it, girl? Have you found something?' He moved her aside to take a closer look. He crouched down beside the box and brushed his hand over it, removing some of the mud that was stuck to it. On the box was a label in capital letters.

'AMSPATRAX TECH CORP...' he whispered.

Below the name was what looked like the outline of a fingertip. Charlie was curious. He was about to wipe the rest of the muck away when Whizzy's voice startled him.

'Hey Charlie, what have you found?'

'Not sure. I found Skyla clawing at it.'

Bridget and Whizzy crouched down beside him, looking intrigued.

'AMSPATRAX TECH CORP.,' Bridget read, wrinkling her nose. 'Never heard of it. Have you?'

Charlie shrugged. Whizzy, on the other hand, looked thoughtful. 'The name rings a bell, but I can't think why.'

'Never mind,' Charlie said and started to brush away the rest of the dirt, revealing a black handprint embedded in the box, along with a small touchscreen, smaller than a pocket calculator. The screen was cracked.

Whizzy's eyes widened. 'Biometric technology HPR!' he said, sounding excited. 'Now that's interesting.'

'What's that in English?' said Bridget.

'Sorry, I mean it's a handprint recognition device,' said Whizzy.

'Okay, so what does one of those do?' Bridget asked.

'Well, biometric technology is designed for security purposes. This one, for instance, requires a person to type a set of numbers on the keypad. While they do that, the code reader analyses their fingerprint. Once that's authenticated, you place your hand in the handprint port, which reads all the main lines, wrinkles and ridges on your hand and fingers. Then, hey presto, the box opens! This type of advanced technology is usually found in areas that require high-level security clearance, such as the White House or NASA, so it's surprising to see it on a box.'

'Unless of course there's something valuable inside the box,' Charlie muttered.

'How do you know all this stuff?' Bridget said, furrowing her brows at Whizzy.

'*Geek-Tech World* on TV – d'you watch it?' Whizzy asked brightly.

'Hello, do I look like the sort of person who spends her time watching a geeky TV channel? No, don't answer that,' Bridget said, shaking her head.

'I'm not judging,' Whizzy responded.

While Whizzy had been explaining HPR, Charlie hadn't taken his eyes off the box – and something strange had been happening. He'd been getting hot and cold flushes. For some mysterious reason, he felt that whatever was locked in the box was calling to him. He felt compelled to place his hand in the security handprint and release it – whatever *it* was. Or perhaps it was all his imagination: there was nothing in the box; he was just curious to see what hidden treasures might await inside. Either way, the temptation was too great to resist. He slid his trembling hand into the handprint. For a moment he felt a tingling of static, as if he were sliding his hand over a television screen. The hairs on the back of his neck stood on end. When nothing else happened, he let out a sigh of disappointment.

'Well, that answers that. It's broken,' he said bitterly.

'Of course, it won't work!' Whizzy rolled his eyes. 'Didn't you listen to what I just said? You have to type in a certain set of numbers, then—'

Suddenly the broken keypad started to spark. Whizzy stopped speaking and the children gasped. Smoke burst from the box. Bridget shrieked as the smoke engulfed them, and they choked and coughed. Meanwhile, Skyla darted off, whining, her tail between her legs. The children stumbled to their feet and ran away from the box, panic-stricken. By the time they came to their senses and turned around, the smoke had dispersed. What they saw came as a real surprise: the box had split in two and lay open on the ground.

None of the children said a word. They stood around the box, exchanging worried looks. But it wasn't long before Charlie cautiously approached the box. Skyla whined and sank her head to the ground.

'Don't, Charlie, don't go near it!' Bridget pleaded.

'It's okay.' Charlie gestured to her. 'I'm just gonna take a quick peek.'

Charlie couldn't see much to begin with, as there was a cloud of smoke still swirling around inside. But the second it evaporated; his anxiety melted away. Inside the padded box was an extraordinary blue crystal encased in a metallic holder. Charlie's eyes widened in astonishment and he gasped. He blinked, then blinked again. After blinking several times, he still couldn't believe what he was staring at.

'What's in there, Charlie? Is it dangerous?' Whizzy yelled.

Before Charlie could answer, there came a heavy *whup-whup-whup*. They looked up to see a black helicopter whiz overhead.

'Well, that sure didn't look like the Forest Rescue chopper,' Bridget said suspiciously.

'Look, it's heading back this way!' Whizzy said.

Charlie turned back to the box. Without thinking, he snatched the crystal and tucked it in the side pocket of his cargo shorts. He turned to the other two, who were still staring at the sky, and said, 'Come on, guys, we better get out of here.'

Skyla leapt to her feet and followed the children as they ran around the plane and over to a nearby bush, where they crouched out of sight. The black helicopter hovered right above the downed plane. It was so loud, it sounded as if it was going to land on top of their heads. Skyla whimpered and crawled between Charlie's legs.

The children peered nervously through the leaves.

To their surprise, they saw five rope lines drop from the helicopter. Five men zipped down to the ground wearing futuristic-looking suits; in them, they looked half human, half machine. Over their black military uniforms, mechanical braces were attached to their spine, so their joints and limbs were operated by levers, pneumatics and hydraulics. They were clearly highly trained and meant business, for they landed with precision, guns drawn. They carried out a sweep of the perimeter and the plane before kneeling around the box. Their faces were concealed by helmets that had dark mirrored visors.

The children gasped.

'Crikey! Their suits look like something out of the future,' said Charlie, gulping.

One of the men, presumably the leader of the team, walked towards the box. His helmet retracted to reveal a middle-aged, bald man with stubble. An earpiece curled around one ear. When he saw that the box was empty, he looked angry. He pressed a button on the forearm of his suit and started speaking.

'What's he saying?' whispered Bridget.

'I ain't gotta clue. I can't hear a thing with all the racket coming from that fricking chopper,' grumbled

Charlie. 'Wait a second – I just remembered something. Whizzy can lip-read!'

Whizzy's sixteen-year-older sister, Jadanna, was deaf, and communicated using sign language and lip reading. Whizzy had learned both.

'Can you read his lips from here?' Charlie asked.

'I can give it a go,' Whizzy stuttered. He squinted through his thick-framed glasses, then whispered to the others.

'He's saying, Alpha Charlie, this is Ghost Team Leader One, do you read me?'

There was a pause while he waited for a reply.

'Affirmative, boss. We've located the transport plane. I can confirm it has been shot down en route to your lab facility. Over.' The man paused again, touching his earpiece, then spoke. 'Negative. We don't know who shot it down. I had a call from base to say the pilot claimed to have seen a black spaceship heading towards them. Over.' The man paused again. 'I doubt it's the Russians, boss – they wouldn't have been stupid enough if they knew what was on board. We've recovered the black box it has been compromised – it's wide open on the ground. There's no sign of Blue Star. I repeat, there's no sign of Blue Star. The pilot is missing; the cockpit has broken off from the fuselage and we haven't located it yet. Over.'

It was not easy for Whizzy to interpret what the man was saying, but he did his best.

'Copy that. I'll have a stealth team dispatched on the ground right away to find the Blue Star – they won't leave a stone unturned. Ghost Team Leader One, over and out!' The man turned to the others and yelled, 'Ghost Team, let's go!'

As the men were about to leave, Bridget accidentally stood on a branch, which snapped. She clapped her hand to her mouth. 'Sorry!' she squeaked.

Charlie shook his head disapprovingly. He didn't think the men would have heard the sound, given the clattering coming from the rotating blades. But he was wrong. He turned back and stared through the leaves. Horror filled his eyes. The soldier who was closest to them was aiming their gun in their direction. He started out towards them, moving stealthily, but by the time he came around the side of the bush, the children and Skyla had fled into the woods. The solider gazed into the forest before heading back to the others.

The children ran headlong through the forest for as long as they could, desperate to escape from the scary men in black. Eventually they slowed to a walk, tired, thirsty and flushed. Even though they'd covered some distance, every so often they glanced back over their shoulder to reassure themselves they weren't being followed.

'That was crazy. I've never seen anything like it!' Whizzy could barely catch his breath.

'Do you think they saw us?' said Bridget, wringing her hands.

'If they did, it'd be your fault,' Charlie said crossly.

'Hey, that's not fair, it was an accident!' said Bridget.

'Still your fault,' he replied.

'Screw you, Charlie Sprewell. I didn't want to go down there in the first place!' Bridget marched ahead.

'Whatever,' Charlie muttered under his breath. He turned to Whizzy, who was staring at him. 'What? She asked for that.'

Whizzy shook his head disapprovingly. 'You should really think before you open your mouth sometimes,' he said, and jogged ahead to catch Bridget up.

'Oh, that's fine, walk with her – see if I care!' Charlie said, in a temper. 'At least I can count on you, Skyla.' Skyla padded along beside him, looking tired, her tongue lolling.

Bridget and Whizzy quietly spoke about Charlie while he followed them, his head bowed. Then Bridget suddenly halted and spun around. A startled Charlie jumped back.

'You know, me and Whizzy were just saying how we should go to the police and tell them what's happened. Do you agree?'

Charlies face turned pale. 'Er, I don't think we should...'

'Oh, really? Why?' Bridget asked.

'Because...' stuttered Charlie. Involuntarily, he touched his pocket over the crystal. His hand tingled, as it had when he first touched the box.

Bridget narrowed her eyes at him. 'What did you take from that box, Charlie?' she demanded.

Charlie tried his best to look innocent, but it was difficult. Bridget could read him like a book. 'Me? What makes you think *I* took something?'

'Because I know you better than you know yourself, and I know when you're lying because your eye twitches,' she said.

'The box was empty. Whizzy told us, remember?' Charlie protested.

'WRONG! Whizzy said the man's words were "it's been taken",' said Bridget, looking irate.

'It is possible I may have made a mistake,' Whizzy said. 'I mean, the guy was a fair distance away.'

'Nevertheless...' Bridget said, looking back at Charlie. 'Well?'

Charlie stood there in silence.

'Fine,' said Bridget, storming off.

Charlie looked at Whizzy.

'You may want to rethink that, mate, because you know where she's heading,' Whizzy said.

Charlie chased Bridget and stopped in front of her. 'Okay, okay, just wait a second, would you?' he said.

'You better tell me right now or else...' Bridget demanded.

'Alright! If I tell you, will you promise me you won't flip and go to the police?' said Charlie.

Bridget folded her arms and raised her eyebrow at him.

Charlie cast a suspicious look at the surrounding forest. 'You're right – there was something in the box.'

'I knew it!' exclaimed Bridget.

'What was it, Charlie?' asked Whizzy curiously.

'Shhh! Keep your voices down. We need to get out of the forest first and back to one of our houses. My house is busy – Mom has some friends over, so that's no good,' Charlie said.

'Mine's free!' Whizzy said. 'The rents are out all day.'

Charlie and Whizzy lived on opposite sides of the same street, and it was quicker to get to their houses from the forest than to Bridget's. The boys loved to hang out at Bridget's house whenever they could as she had a swimming pool.

'Your house it is,' said Charlie, and the four of them made their way back as quickly as they could.

CHAPTER 3

FINDERS, KEEPERS

Back at Whizzy's house, the children grabbed cold drinks from the kitchen, including Skyla, who drank thirstily from a bowl of water Charlie gave her. Once satisfied, they headed off to Whizzy's bedroom, which was in the basement. It was lovely and cool in Whizzy's bedroom, as always.

'I wonder what happened to the pilot?' said Whizzy as he marched down the stairs.

'I doubt he's alive,' said Charlie, following the other two.

'You sound as if you don't care what happened to him, Charlie,' Bridget commented.

'Nah. I'm just saying, I'd be surprised if anyone was able to walk away from the crash.' Charlie frowned.

They grabbed chairs and sat around the small table in Whizzy's room. Whizzy's bedroom was like a space museum. It was full of posters of space, with space mobiles dangling from the ceiling, crazy gadgets that lit up, and weird inventions that Whizzy had designed himself. But none of that was the least bit interesting to the children right now. They were there to see what Charlie was guarding in his side pocket, which he had done all the way home from the forest.

'Alright, Charlie, spill it!' Bridget ordered, clearly still annoyed at him. 'What did you take from the box that those crazy people had come for?'

Charlie smirked at the pair. 'This!' he said and laid the magnificent blue crystal on the table.

'Jeez, would you look at that?' Whizzy said, his eyes almost popping out of his head.

'Charlie!' was the only word Bridget could bring herself to muster.

'I know, right? It's pretty awesome, isn't it?' Charlie said, grinning proudly.

'I can't believe you stole that – what on earth were you thinking?' Bridget said.

Charlie's face fell. 'Wait, what?' He scratched his head in confusion.

'I think what Bridget is trying to say, Charlie, is that those dangerous-looking guys with masks and guns were sent to recover this magnificent – and very expensive-looking – blue crystal – but you, in your great wisdom, decided to steal it from them. And lord only knows what they will do to us if they find out we have it. Does that sound about right, Bridget?' Whizzy asked.

'I couldn't have said it better myself,' said Bridget.

'You're welcome.' Whizzy nodded, gratified.

'But, guys, they don't know we have it, and what about the old saying, "Finders, keepers, losers, weepers"? We found it, so we should get to keep it, right?' said Charlie.

'Charlie does make a sensible argument,' said Whizzy, stroking his chin in a thoughtful manner. 'We have found things in the past that we've laid claim to.'

'Thank you!' said Charlie. 'At last someone around here can see sense.'

'That's different,' said Bridget.

'How?' asked Charlie, feeling that the argument was starting to turn in his favour.

'Because things we've found in the past have never been worth a dime! Plus, in order for the ancient Roman law to apply, this...' – Bridget pointed at the crystal – 'needs to be lost and hidden for a considerable length of time in order for us to make a claim against it, but this doesn't apply here, because you stole it from a plane that crashed only moments ago!'

'And there it is – game, set and match, ladies and gentlemen,' said Whizzy. Charlie said nothing. He leaned back in his chair in a huff.

'Though I will say, Charlie, it is the most remarkable crystal I've ever seen,' Whizzy said, inspecting it closely. The inside of the crystal swirled around like the cosmos.

'Look, Charlie, what you did is wrong. I suggest we take the crystal to the police station and hand in right away,' Bridget said, folding her arms.

Charlie didn't want to admit it, but deep down he knew Bridget was right. It bordered on theft, and he certainly did not want to be labelled a thief. He sighed. 'You're right. I shouldn't have taken it. I'll go there now and tell them...'

He stopped short.

He couldn't believe his eyes.

Whizzy was holding out his finger, almost touching the crystal. Incredibly, a blue and white electrical energy streamed out from the crystal, connecting to his fingertip.

Charlie's mouth fell open, and he lurched forward in his chair. 'How are you doing that?'

'I have no idea! It just happens when you hold your finger near it,' said Whizzy.

'Here, let me try!' said Charlie. Nervously, he placed his hand over the crystal and watched in awe as streams of plasma light connected with his fingers. It was like watching a miniature lightning storm arching from the sky to the ground. Charlie clasped the crystal and felt energy surge through his body. The hairs on the back of his neck stood on end. It felt as though the crystal was charging him up. The crystal also seemed to react to Charlie – it grew brighter.

'Whoa, I can feel this crazy rush of energy from the crystal. It, like, makes me wanna go running, super-fast!' Charlie was full of excitement.

They all stared at the crystal, nonplussed, then something even stranger happened. The table started to shake, and the floor started to vibrate dramatically. The room grew darker. Skyla awoke with a start, scrambled from underneath the table and scarpered up the stairs. Bridget and Whizzy turned pale with fright. Charlie's expression had changed: it had become serious. His complexion darkened, the veins in his neck and face bulged a bright blue, and sparks of electricity crawled across his skin.

'Er, Charlie, something's happening to you, you might wanna let go of that thing!' Bridget pleaded with him.

'Yeah, mate, let go of it, you're freaking us out!' Whizzy leaned back in his chair, away from Charlie, and grabbed Bridget's arm.

Charlie couldn't hear them. His attention was focused on the crystal. 'It's calling to me,' he said, his voice deeper than usual.

Suddenly, Charlie's eyes turned a gleaming black. Bridget let out a hysterical scream and kicked the table away. The table struck Charlie's hand and sent the crystal soaring through the air. It flew across the bedroom and hit the wall, bounced off a space globe and landed in Whizzy's waste bin. Everything returned to normal, including Charlie, who looked dazed. Bridget and Whizzy looked as if they had just got off a terrifying fairground ride. They sat gawping at Charlie, who eventually came round. He shook his head, as if to clear it.

'What's wrong with you guys, and why's the table on the floor?' he asked.

'You wouldn't believe us if we told you,' Whizzy squeaked.

'Charlie – your nose! It's bleeding!' said Bridget in a trembling voice.

Charlie wiped it. To his alarm, he saw bright red blood on his fingers, and ran out of the room to the bathroom. He soon returned, tissue stuck up his nostrils, to see Bridget and Whizzy looking apprehensive.

'Are you alright, Charlie?' Bridget asked quietly.

'Yeah, I'm fine. Just a little nosebleed – probably caused by the pollen from the woods or something,' Charlie replied.

'But you don't suffer from hay fever. I do!' Whizzy said, looking nervously between Bridget and Charlie.

Charlie shrugged. 'I don't know, then.'

'I think we'd better discuss what just happened,' said Bridget.

They picked the table up and sat back round it again. It didn't take the children long to explain to Charlie what happened. As they told him, he sat silently, a dumbstruck look upon his face.

'I can't believe it. Are you sure that's what really happened? I don't remember a thing. One minute I was talking to you guys, the next I was running out the door,' said Charlie.

'Oh, it happened alright!' Whizzy said reassuringly.

'So where's the thing now?' asked Charlie, looking around.

Bridget turned to look over her shoulder. 'It's over there.'

The three of them got up and slowly approached the bin. They gazed nervously down at the blue crystal lying at the bottom.

'I don't know what that thing is, but it's bad news, I tell you,' said Bridget. 'Your head looked like it was going to explode!' She walked over to Whizzy's bed and sat down. Meanwhile, Skyla came creeping back down the stairs. She sat between Bridget's legs and draped her head over Bridget's thigh. Bridget stroked her gently.

'You're telling me.' Whizzy fidgeted with his glasses – he did this when he was nervous. 'You looked like that guy from *Spider-Man* – what's his name?'

'Dr Octopus?' guessed Charlie.

'No, not him,' said Whizzy.

'Green Goblin?'

'No, the one who turns blue and is full of electric!'

'Electro?' Charlie guessed again.

'That's him! Electro! You looked like him, except you didn't look like you had special powers. You looked more like you were going to explode, like Bridget said.' Whizzy slumped down into his chair at his computer desk.

'I get it. I'm sorry – what do you want me to say? I didn't know that was going to happen,' Charlie said.

'How d'you feel now?' asked Whizzy.

'Fine.' Charlie shrugged. 'But the way it made me feel when I touched it – its energy, its, its power, its—'

'It's dangerous, that's what it is!' Bridget interjected. 'And it could have seriously hurt you, or even killed you! We need to get rid of it ASAP!'

Charlie paused to think. 'From what you've said, you're right. It's too dangerous for it to be here in Cravins…'

'Never mind in my house!' cried Whizzy. 'It could've blown the place up! I'm in enough trouble as it is with my folks because the soap powder dispenser, I invented malfunctioned in the garage last week. The last thing I need is the crystal blowing up the house.'

Bridget tittered.

'I do think, before we hand it in, perhaps we should find out who it belongs to, just in case…' Charlie said, half expecting Bridget to knock back his suggestion.

'Why am I sensing you're up to something?' said Bridget, pressing her lips firmly together.

'So, is that a yes?' asked Charlie, raising an eyebrow.

'On one condition…'

'Name it,' said Charlie.

'After we find out who it belongs to, we go straight to the police and tell them everything that's happened, otherwise you can count me out!' Bridget said adamantly.

'Deal,' replied Charlie. 'Whizzy?'

'I don't see what harm it can do. I'm in,' Whizzy said in a calm voice.

'Great! Let's see what we can dig up then,' said Charlie, smiling and rubbing his hands together.

'So, where do we start?' Whizzy asked.

CHAPTER 4

A GAME OF WAR

'First things first: we need to lock that thing away before it does any more harm to either of us. You got anything we can use, Whizzy?' Charlie said, looking around his bedroom.

'Not in here,' said Whizzy. 'I'll go take a quick look in the garage. Dad's bound to have something lying around in there we can use.'

'No, I'll go!' Bridget said, leaping eagerly from the bed. 'You boys can stay here and babysit that thing. I don't want to be anywhere near it. C'mon, Skyla.'

'Whatever you do, make sure you DON'T – TOUCH – THE – POWDER – DISPENSING – MACHINE! THANK YOU!' Whizzy shouted. He turned to Charlie, to see him looking deep in thought. By now he'd pulled the tissues from his nose and was twiddling the ends with his fingers. 'You okay, Charlie?'

'Am, Amtis ... no, that's not it,' he said, shaking his head in frustration. 'Darn, what was the name of it?'

'What are you trying to do, Charlie?' Whizzy asked, swivelling from side to side in his chair.

'I'm trying to remember the name that was written on the box I found the crystal in. You don't remember, do you?' Charlie asked.

A few seconds later, Whizzy lunged forward in his chair. 'Amspatrax!'

'That's it!' said Charlie. 'Now, see what you can find on your computer under that name.'

'I'm on it!' Whizzy said, tapping away at the keyboard while Charlie paced the bedroom, biting his lip.

A short while later, Skyla came bounding down the stairs followed by Bridget, holding a small lockable tin and a pair of rubber gloves.

'What are those for?' Charlie enquired.

'It's called precaution. After seeing what that thing did to you, I ain't touching it!' Bridget said, slipping one of the gloves on. 'Oh, and by the way, Whizzy, your garage is full of soap again.'

'WHAT!'

'I'm just kidding.' She giggled.

Whizzy groaned. 'That's not funny, Bridge.'

'The look of panic on your face was funny,' she said.

Whizzy shook his head and went back to the keyboard.

Charlie slipped the other glove on. Cautiously, he approached the bin, picked it up carefully and tipped the crystal into the box which Bridget was holding open. She slammed the lid shut, turned the key and placed it in her jeans pocket. Bridget sighed. 'That's a relief.'

'Guys come here. I think I've found something!' Whizzy said, beckoning them over.

Charlie and Bridget gathered round and stared at the monitor, which showed an image of a space shuttle.

An angry look flared in Charlie's eye. 'Argh, Whizzy, we ain't got time to be looking at one of your stupid space sites right now – we need to find out about this fricking crystal!'

'That's what I've been doing! I'm trying to show you. Look!' Whizzy pointed to the name at the top of the screen.

'America Space Travel and Exploration,' Bridget read out. 'I don't get it.'

'Don't you see? The first few letters from each word make up a name – the name we're searching for! AMSPATRAX!' said Whizzy.

'Oh yeah!' exclaimed Charlie.

'I knew I'd seen the name somewhere before,' Whizzy said, clicking his fingers.

'So, the crystal belongs to a space company?' said Bridget, looking at the boys.

'I'd say the person who owns the space exploration company owns the blue crystal, and that would be this – man – right – here!' Whizzy clicked on the About tab on the page. An image of a slender, clean-shaven man flashed up. He wore a black suit, and his dark hair was slicked back. Behind him was a space rocket.

Charlie brought his face closer to the screen. 'Who's that guy?' he said, wrinkling his nose.

'That, ladies and gentlemen, is the billionaire Enoch Salvador, the owner of America Space Travel and Exploration!' Whizzy said with reverence. 'He's a pioneer. He's built a super-intelligent computer called A.L.I.C.E. It says here that his company, Amspatrax Tech Corp., is the leading private organisation in space exploration and technologies, and the only company to offer people a ride around the Earth in a rocket. I met him a couple of years ago at the World Science Festival, where he was giving a talk about the new technologies his company had created and the missions his team have been on in space. He said that he was looking forward to going up for the first time with members of the public in the Viking X1 space rocket. Man, what I'd give for a ride in that!'

'Sounds to me like someone's got a crush on this guy,' Bridget said, nudging Charlie and winking.

Charlie sniggered.

'Pfft, I wouldn't expect either of you two to appreciate a genius even if you saw one in the flesh,' Whizzy said defensively.

'You're right – I don't see one round here in the flesh!' Bridget laughed.

'Cut it out, you guys, and get serious, would you?' Charlie said, sounding annoyed. 'If we're assuming this Salvador guy is the owner of the blue crystal, we need to know more about him and what he's up to. Whizzy, what else do you know about him?'

Whizzy did a quick search, then pulled up a news article dated a decade ago and read the headline aloud. '"US Government Pulls the Plug on Funding Enoch Salvador's Military Exosuit Programme, condemning the suits as unreliable and a waste of money after a series of failures".'

'Seems like this guy has a finger in everything,' Bridget commented.

Whizzy scrolled down the article, and a small image caught Charlie's eye. 'Wait a second, Whizzy – click on that, would you?' he said, pointing to it.

Whizzy clicked on the image. It was of a man in a familiar black camouflage military uniform.

'Jeez, that looks like the same uniform as those men wore in the forest!' Whizzy said, staring at the screen, 'except theirs looked like more advanced.'

'I agree and look at what it says here.' Charlie pointed to the caption underneath the photo. '"A prototype of the military stealth exoskeleton suit!"'

'Clearly the US government didn't pull the plug on the programme after all,' said Bridget, 'but what does the blue crystal have to do with all this?'

'There's only one way to find out.' Whizzy smiled, cracking his fingers.

Charlie and Bridget ignored Whizzy as he typed a ton of coding stuff that neither of them knew anything about. All they knew was that he was hacking into something.

'Have you found anything yet?' Charlie asked anxiously, biting his thumbnail.

Whizzy shook his head. 'This is not good enough, Whizzy, you should've been in by now' he muttered, redoubling his efforts.

'Is he talking to himself?' Bridget whispered into Charlie's ear. 'You know that's the first sign of madness, right?'

'Especially when he starts referring to himself in the third person,' Charlie said out of the corner of his mouth.

A minute or two later, Whizzy clapped his hands and shrieked with delight. 'BOOM! I'm in. Phew, that was a tough one, but you can't keep the king of hacking out.'

'Alright, cool. So what are we looking at?' Charlie said, pulling up a seat alongside him.

'Okay, so to keep it simple, I have managed to hack into Amspatrax Tech Corp.'s operating system, which was pretty difficult,' Whizzy said quickly.

'Ooh, how much trouble will we be in for doing this?' Bridget looked worried.

'A truck-load,' Whizzy replied, looking at her over his glasses, 'but only if we get caught, so we need to be super-quick before they realise someone's snooping around in their backyard.'

'Well, I suggest we be more than super-quick!' Bridget said, gesturing for him to hurry.

Whizzy got to work opening and closing files: ANCINV-1, PIMD, BDH11, COVID... The information in them didn't make any sense to the children; it all seemed to be related to viruses. Other files were related to military and space programmes. Time was ticking on, and they were having no luck at finding anything. The children were about to give up when Whizzy stumbled upon a file named PROJECT R. He clicked on it. The file opened. It contained a list of hundreds of files, each marked with a number.

'What are all these?' Charlie said curiously.

'I'm not sure...' replied Whizzy.

He clicked on the most recent file, marked 'LOG 968 – Robonik'. The children were surprised to see that it was a video of Enoch Salvador dressed in a white lab coat.

Whizzy clicked the play button and the video started. Salvador sat on a stool facing the camera. He seemed to be in a high-tech laboratory. Opera music played in the background. Salvador gave a command to A.L.I.C.E., his highly sophisticated computer, to mute the music before he spoke calmly into the camera.

'Hey, you guys, that's his supercomputer I was telling you about!' said Whizzy excitedly.

'That's great, Whizzy, let's listen,' said Charlie.

Whizzy frowned.

'Enoch Salvador log nine six eight. Date, July twenty-first, 2005—'

'That's only a few days ago!' exclaimed Charlie.

'The time is...' Salvador glanced at his expensive watch. 'Zero four hundred hours PST. Today we have made the biggest technological breakthrough technology since computers were invented.

'Ten years ago the foolish, short-sighted American government decided to withdraw its funding to my military exosuit programme, when we were on the brink of successfully launching the MK2 stealth exosuit. They made a fool out of me! Fortunately, all was not lost, for someone else saw the potential in my exosuit programme: a military leader by the name of Vladimir Isakov. After seeing the results, he was more than willing to invest. Of course, in return for his generous investment he received the first orders of MK2 tactical suits, along with MK3s, in 2003.

'Right now, my team are trialling the latest version, the MK4, but we have yet to ship these to our investors in Russia. This is because of the increasing sanctions placed on Russia by our government. These sanctions are good for business, as they will lead to further tension between our countries. And when war breaks out between the two – a war I intend to initiate – this will create a huge demand for my exosuits. As the English say, where there's muck there's brass. I intend to be right in the middle, orchestrating it all with my latest weapon design.

'But before I unveil my technological masterpiece, I want to talk about the monumental discovery made by my team of explorers on their recent secret mission to an unknown planet in the Xia solar system. It seems we may not be alone in the universe after all. One of the crew members of the Viking X2 claimed that he saw an extraterrestrial life form while returning to the space shuttle with the extraordinary object they had discovered. However, his sighting could not be substantiated as the party was behind schedule to depart the planet. But, as to what they returned with ... words fail to describe how remarkable it is. We call it the Blue Star.'

The children exchanged astonished looks and kept on watching.

'It looks like a crystal. However, when we compared its composition to the minerals we have here on Earth, we found that this foreign object is unlike any crystals we know. For the past month, my team of scientists have carried out vigorous testing. The Blue Star is resistant to everything but one thing. Humans. It appears that this object, which has come from the far reaches of space, reacts to human contact. We made this unfortunate discovery by chance when one of my scientists picked it up without wearing protective clothing. They could not let go of the Blue Star after they had picked it up, and moments later, they died, tragically.

'Since then we have come up with two theories: one, that the Blue Star is piezoelectric. When a human comes into contact with the Blue Star, it generates an electric charge. But the tests we ran to try to prove this were inconclusive. So that leads us to our second theory: that the Blue Star is a kind of symbiote. It attaches itself to a host and passes its energy through them. However, as the unfortunate scientist who came into physical contact with the Blue Star found out, this energy is too much for humans to cope with. But all is not lost – and I, genius that I am, have found a solution to this problem.'

Salvador sprang off the stool with the energy of a child and hurried over to the centre of the room, where a raised hexagonal platform stood, surrounded by soft turquoise lights.

Salvador commanded A.L.I.C.E. to change to aircam. Within seconds a white ball with a bulbous built-in lens floated in the air.

Charlie was perturbed by Salvador's behaviour. What was he up to now? But he also wanted to know what the solution was.

'What I'm about to show you is the most advanced piece of technology to ever exist. It is the Holy Grail in technology, it is a game-changer. It will change how we wage war. A.L.I.C.E., would you please reveal Robonik?' Salvador commanded.

A.L.I.C.E. carried out the order. A plume of ice-cold air shot up from the hexagonal platform. From it, a large glass cylindrical section rose high into the air and docked with the ceiling. Suspended inside was an extraordinary suit.

The boys were mesmerised by the black suit with the diamond-shaped mesh, but Bridget didn't share their enthusiasm. She sniggered, drawing a sharp look from the boys.

'What? It looks like a black leotard, if you ask me,' she remarked. The boys shook their heads and swiftly turned back to the screen.

Salvador stood gazing in admiration at his creation. 'Magnificent, isn't it? Robonik is the only exosuit in the world that is made from nanotechnology using nitinol and a special material, dyanik.'

'I vaguely recall him mentioning nanotechnology and this dyanik material at that science festival. He said it would revolutionise industry and be used for ground-breaking experiments,' Whizzy murmured.

'Now you know what he's using it for,' commented Charlie.

'Now, the MK4 stealth exosuit you see here,' Salvador said, walking over to a life-sized mannequin wearing the suit, 'includes mechanical braces attached to the spine, hips and limbs of soldiers. These are designed to enhance their physical abilities. The suit requires battery packs, and this is their greatest downside – the batteries need to be charged or replaced frequently. But the nanotechnology in the Robonik exosuit has been designed to do away with all the physical attachments of the previous suits, which place a strain on the body and use far more human energy. As we know, the human body can produce enough electrical energy to power a small lightbulb—'

'That's true,' Whizzy said, nodding.

'However, our bodies cannot produce enough electrical energy to charge up a suit of this size – but, with the Blue Star's help, I believe we can. Think of the Blue Star as being a power source for the body: it can generate limitless amounts of energy, all the energy we need to electrically charge the millions of nanobots in the Robonik exosuit. And this neurocranial transmitter, which I've created and built into this helmet,' Salvador said, showing the camera, 'connects my brain with the smartest, most sophisticated thinking machine on the planet—'

'THANK YOU, DR SALVADOR,' replied a soft, womanly robotic voice.

'You're most welcome, A.L.I.C.E.,' Salvador said modestly. 'In this way, I will have complete mind control over the nanobots. The Robonik suit will give me unprecedented strength and agility and is impenetrable to weapons. I will become the ultimate superhuman.

'Once the Blue Star has been flown to my personal lab from the other facility, we will begin Phase 1 of testing. I have no doubt that I will be able to harness the Blue Star's power using the Robonik suit. And when I do, I'll start a war with Russia, making it look as if the US government has targeted them. When they retaliate, our pathetic government will have no choice but to come grovelling back to me, begging me to build suits for the US army – with an open chequebook. They will come to regret the day they tried to reject and humiliate me.' Salvador stared darkly into the camera with an evil grin.

Suddenly the screen went blank.

'Uh, what's happened to the video?' Charlie said.

Frantically, Whizzy raced to re-establish a connection, but despite his best efforts he was unable to. 'Damn it!' he said.

'They found out, didn't they?' asked Bridget.

'Yep, they sure did. As I said, we needed to be quick. They've ejected us from their systems. There's no way of getting back in – well, not at the moment anyway.' Whizzy scratched his head in frustration.

'It doesn't matter. We saw enough to know what this Salvador guy's up to; you did good,' Charlie said, patting him on the back.

Whizzy half smiled.

'Yeah, enough to know that he wants to start World War Three with us and the Russians! Huh, there'll be no more *Bonnie and the Dream Team* when that happens, and just when I was about to find out whether Matias was going to ask Bonnie to be his girlfriend.' Bridget sighed dreamily.

'Actually, Salvador can't start a thing. Are you guys forgetting what we have of his?' Charlie said, pointing behind him. They turned to stare at the tin box on the table.

'Good point, but what are we gonna to do with it now?' Whizzy said, leaning back in his chair and linking his hands behind his head.

'Hang on, didn't we agree to take it to the police once we found out who it belongs to?' Bridget said.

Charlie exhaled. 'We did, but how are we gonna explain to them how we came by it or how we've obtained the information on Salvador without getting into trouble?'

'Charlie's right, Bridge. We can't exactly tell the police we hacked into Amspatrax's systems, can we?' Whizzy added.

'We need proof, otherwise they'll just see us as crazy kids looking for attention,' said Charlie.

Bridget stomped around the room in a huff. 'I knew I shouldn't have listened to you,' she complained, running her fingers through her hair. 'So now what?'

Charlie gazed out through the small, dusty windows. The room had grown dim in the time they'd been there.

'I dunno. But I do know that my stomach feels like a ravenous bear right now. I can't think straight,' he said, rubbing it absentmindedly.

'Now that you come to mention it, I do believe a bowl of gumbo would go down well right now,' said Whizzy, licking his lips.

'Well, that's just great. We've got a predicament on our hands and all you boys can think about is your flaming stomachs!' Bridget said, shaking her head and rolling her eyes.

'Well, they do say good decisions are often made after a good meal,' Whizzy pointed out.

'Look, Skyla's gonna need feeding anyway, so I suggest we pick this up tomorrow. Let's meet first thing at my house so we can figure this out,' Charlie said.

They carried out their group handshake, involving a fist bump, elbow knock and hand wiggling, before they clattered up the creaky stairs. Whizzy saw them to the back door via the kitchen, where they parted. Charlie and Bridget headed down the drive.

The sun had started to sink beyond the woods of Cravins Creek, but since it was August it was still wonderfully warm out. Skyla padded slowly beside Charlie. After passing five or six houses, the children reached Charlie's house, on the opposite side of the road.

'Catch you later, bubblehead!' said Charlie as he jogged across the road with Skyla.

'See you tomorrow, pea-brain!' replied Bridget, continuing to walk briskly.

As Charlie ran across his lawn, he involuntarily glanced up the road. He was surprised to see an unfamiliar black van parked there. He slowed to a stop, gazing at the van, which had blacked-out windows. He couldn't recall ever seeing it before. He looked over at Bridget, who by now was almost out of view.

Then his stomach growled again. Charlie brushed aside his suspicions and continued into his house.

CHAPTER 5

SHAWN GREEN

After eating supper, Charlie retired to his bedroom to watch baseball on TV. He lay on his bed, casually tossing a baseball into the air and catching it in his glove. Since arriving home he'd been feeling odd. He'd been experiencing a sort of fuzzy sensation, as if he'd forgotten to do something. Suddenly it dawned on him. A streak of panic flashed before his eyes and he sat bolt upright in bed. He had left the Blue Star at Whizzy's house, on the table. With all the excitement of the day, it'd simply slipped his mind.

Before he had a chance to go downstairs to ring Whizzy, there was a knock on his bedroom door, then it creaked open.

'Hey, sport,' said a cheery voice.

It was Charlie's mom's partner, Evan McGruff. Evan was a tall beefy man with a scruffy beard. He was a long-distance truck driver. Charlie thought a lot of Evan. He was a humble, kind man who treated his mom and him with respect and never tried to replace his dad. But what really brought the pair closer together was their shared passion for baseball. They had a friendly rivalry going. Charlie was a huge fan of the Los Angeles Dodgers, and his bedroom was full of his team's memorabilia. Evan, on the other hand, was a lifelong fan of the San Francisco Giants. He came into Charlie's room wearing his usual tatty grey Giants cap.

Charlie lay back on his bed and pretended to act normal, although he was dying to speak to Whizzy.

'Hey, Evan.'

'So how's the game going? Who's winning?' Evan asked politely, hovering in the doorway.

'Good. Shannings got two RBIs for the Dodgers, but was thrown out at third,' said Charlie.

Evan wrinkled his forehead. 'Humph, he's not bad for a lefty, I'll give him that,' he said teasingly.

'Wha'ever,' Charlie said, rising to the bait. 'You know he was the MVP last year, and the only player to smash Shawn Green's record of four home runs in a game playing for the Dodgers, and the guy's only twenty-two!'

Evan's broad shoulders bobbed up and down as he chuckled to himself. 'You keep hitting the way you do, and you'll be the next Shawn Green,' he said, wagging his finger at him. 'Hey, listen...' He poked his head back round the landing before quietly closing the door and taking a seat on the end of Charlie's bed, almost squashing Skyla in the process, who was sprawled out at the end, whimpering in her sleep. 'How'd you like to go to a game with me next Saturday? I managed to score two tickets,' he said, pulling them from the back pocket of his faded jeans.

Charlie's eyes lit up with excitement. 'The Dodgers versus the White Sox – are you kidding me! But how did you—'

'Well, you know...' Evan made a fist.

'I thought Mom had banned you from arm wrestling?' Charlie said, raising his eyebrows.

'Shhh, keep your voice down,' Evan warned, pressing his finger to his lips. 'Yeah, that's what your mom thinks. But I've had a couple of easy matches against some chumps – you know how it is, can't have them thinking they're better than me. It's no big deal. Just don't go telling your mom. She'll hit the roof if she finds out and I'll be back sleeping in the spare room again.'

Charlie caught a glimpse of the silver scar on Evan's elbow from the surgery he'd had after breaking his elbow in an arm wrestling match the year before. He remembered how upset his mom had been with Evan – not because he got under her feet for nearly two months while he recovered at home, but because he didn't get paid for the time off work. Since then, Debby had banned Evan from arm wrestling.

Charlie nodded. 'My lips are sealed,' he said, pretending to zip them, 'but what are you gonna to say Mom when she asks where you got the tickets?'

'Don't worry about that. I've got it covered.' Evan gave him a wink and the pair fist-bumped. Evan cleared his throat. 'Hey, listen. There is one other thing I wanted to run by you. I ... er ... I know I'm not your father an' all, and heaven forbid I'm not trying to fill his boots. He sounded like a great guy, and I know how much he meant to your mom and you. But how you feel about him, well...'

Charlie could see how anxious Evan was becoming. He was never one to talk about his feelings. Charlie felt humbled that he was trying to express his affection for him.

'It's okay, I get it,' Charlie said.

Evan cleared his throat again. 'What I'm basically trying to say is, you guys mean a lot to me. I'd like to ask your blessing before I ask your mom to marry me.'

Charlie's jaw dropped. He sat there, speechless, for a second or two without even blinking, then lunged forward and threw his arms around Evan. A happy smile spread across Evan's lips and he gently wrapped his arms around Charlie.

'I would be happy for you to marry Mom,' Charlie said, smiling.

Evan let out a sigh of relief. 'Thanks, kid, that means a lot. Of course, she's gotta say yes first.' They chuckled.

'Let's hope for your sake she does, otherwise you'll be taking a big L!' Charlie said. 'So have you bought a ring for her yet?'

'Well, that's the other thing I wanted to speak to you about. As you know, I'm not much of a jewellery man. If it was left to me, I'd end up giving her a wheel nut from off the truck, so I figured maybe you could come help me pick one out before we go watch the game?' Evan asked.

'I'd love to!' Charlie said excitedly. 'I mean, if it's alright with you?'

'Sure it is,' Evan said, gently rubbing Charlie's shoulder. 'Hey, you'll probably do a far better job than I would of picking one.'

Evan gave a yawn and shook his head. 'Oh, looks like bed's calling. Sorry, sport, I'd love to stay here talking with you all night, but I need to hit the sack. Gotta early start tomorrow. Goodnight, Charlie.' He got up and lumbered to the door.

'Hey, Evan?'

Evan stopped in the doorway and jerked his head around.

'Thanks,' Charlie said with great sincerity, holding up the tickets.

Evan's eyes softened as he smiled. 'You're welcome, sport,' he said, and quietly closed the door behind him.

A split second later, the door swung back open and Evan cheekily popped his head back round again. 'Just so you know, Shannings would do far better if he were playing for the Giants,' he said, grinning.

'Shut up!' Charlie said, slinging his pillow at the door as Evan closed it.

Charlie leaned back against the headboard and stared in amazement at the tickets he held. His heart was thumping with joy. He rarely had the chance to watch his favourite team play, since they lived a gruelling eleven-hour drive from their stadium. But that distance seemed irrelevant now. It could be seven days' travel, for all he cared. He was going to see the Dodgers play and that was all that mattered.

'Did you hear that, Skyla?' he said brightly, looking at her lying at the end of his bed. 'I'm going to see the Dodgers play!'

Skyla's eyelids peeled open. She gave a groan as she stretched, closed her eyes and went back to sleep.

Charlie sat, grinning from ear to ear, staring at the tickets as if they were gold bars, when he heard an echoing clang. It came from outside. He climbed out of bed and made his way to the window to investigate.

It was dark outside; night had fallen. But thankfully the bright street lighting made it possible for him to see the cause of the racket. Over the road, a raccoon dangled from a neighbour's rubbish bin. Its black and white striped tail was a dead giveaway.

Charlie huffed and shook his head. Then out of the corner of his eye he saw a light flicker. By the time he turned his head to look, it had disappeared. Charlie cast his eyes suspiciously at the houses and gardens on the other side of the road. As always, everything appeared perfectly normal in his quiet town.

Perhaps one of the streetlights was on the way out, he thought.

But a few seconds later, it happened again, and this time he caught sight of the light. Six houses down the street, from a dark window on the top floor, a tiny light flickered. Of course, this wasn't any random house; it was Whizzy's house.

Charlie waited anxiously a while longer, to be sure it wasn't someone fooling around. But after several seconds, when the tiny light flashed from the window, there was no doubt in Charlie's mind: there was an emergency of some kind and Whizzy was trying to reach out to him.

Worry uncoiled in Charlie's stomach. He had been so overcome with Evan's news that he'd forgotten about the Blue Star over at Whizzy's – again. He raced around the room, looking for his walkie-talkie. He had no idea where he'd seen it last and finally happened to stumble upon it in a pile of rubbish underneath his bed. The second he switched it on and turned up the volume, out came Whizzy's voice, blaring like a tannoy announcement in a supermarket.

'WHIZZY TO SLUGGER, ARE YOU THERE? COME IN, COME IN!'

'Slugger to Whizzy, I'm here. I read you loud and clear, over!' Charlie responded, bolting back to his window to signal back with his torch.

'About time! I've only been trying to get hold of you for, like, the entire evening on the radio!' Whizzy sounded frustrated.

'Sorry, mate, I haven't had my walkie switched on the past few days,' Charlie replied, staring down the street. 'Anyway, is everything alright? Has something happened to the You-Know-What? Over.'

'You mean the You-Know-What you forgot to take with you!' Whizzy said curtly.

'Yeah, sorry about that.'

'It's fine,' Whizzy said.

'Oh, good!' Charlie said, relieved to hear it. 'So what's the matter then? You know we only use the window signal in emergencies when we can't leave the house or use the phone to get hold of each other, right?'

'Yes, I'm perfectly aware, which is why I've been trying to reach you on the radio. There's a problem,' said Whizzy.

'Look, if this is about that new invention of yours, I'm not interested.' Charlie turned back to check the score on TV. 'Whatever it is, can't it wait until tomorrow? I'm trying to watch the game.' He rolled his eyes.

'NO, IT CAN'T WAIT TIL TOMORROW!'

Charlie jerked his head away from the radio, deafened. 'Alright, Whizzy, calm down, there's no need to get your panties in a bunch.'

'Then listen to me, would you? This is serious.' Whizzy's tone was brusque.

'Well, if it was, why didn't you just ring me? It would've been far easier than standing in the window all night flashing a torch,' Charlie suggested. This only seemed to work Whizzy up into more of a frenzy.

'Because my telephone might be bugged and that means someone might be listening in on our conversation, that's why. OVER!' Whizzy hissed.

'Bugged?' Charlie muttered. 'Whizzy, what on earth are you talking about? What do you mean, your phone's bugged? Over.'

'Look, I can't say any more over the comms. Meet me at the park at twenty-one twenty hours. I'll explain there. Over,' Whizzy said in a slightly calmer tone.

This didn't sound good, Charlie thought. If the children were ever in danger, they arranged to meet at 'the park'– but 'the park' was code, in case someone was ever tracking them. It meant their secret hideout. Something was seriously wrong. Charlie knew how much Whizzy hated the dark, but he was the one calling the emergency meeting.

Charlie threw a glance at his baseball clock on the side table. It was nine o'clock. His mom would be going to bed soon, so it shouldn't be too hard for him to sneak out of the house.

'Is Ryder meeting us there, over?' Charlie questioned. Ryder was Bridget's CB handle – she had named herself after her pony.

'Negative. I've tried reaching her this evening, but I've had no luck. Over,' replied Whizzy.

'Knowing her, she's probably stuffing her face with ice cream and watching that stupid TV show,' Charlie joked.

'Copy that. See you at the rendezvous point in twenty minutes. Slugger over and out.'

Charlie stood for a moment gazing absentmindedly out the window, wondering what could possibly be so urgent that they had to meet at that time of night.

He stuffed his pillows under his quilt to make it look as though he was in bed, in case his mom came in, switched his TV off and pulled a hoodie from his closet. He slipped it on and zipped it up over his navy T-shirt. Skyla leapt off the bed and followed Charlie to the door.

'Uh-uh, not you, girl, you're staying put,' he said to her, flicking the bedroom light off. Skyla whined as he slipped out and quietly closed the door behind him.

CHAPTER 6

THE SECRET HIDEOUT

Charlie stood by a chain-link fence. On the other side was Cravins Creek Forest. Instead of carrying on into the woods, he hesitated and glanced up at the starry sky. The moon was almost full. Charlie felt on edge. The fable about the Red Lady of Cravins Creek played on his mind.

The story took place over one hundred years ago. Cheryl Sasmia had gone for a walk through Cravins Creek Forest one day and had never returned. For days people searched the forest but there was no sign of her. From then, stories about her disappearance emerged and over time these stories became twisted. Charlie was reminded of how the Red Lady would float through the forest at night, wearing a white dress drenched in her own blood ... when the moon was full.

Some of the locals Charlie had spoken to over the years claimed to have seen the lost soul of the young lady searching for her way home, and warned anyone foolish enough to be in the woods on the night of the full moon that they would suffer a terrible fate, should they come into contact with her.

Charlie didn't believe in ghosts, but it didn't stop him from seeking reassurance either. After seeing the bright moon, he finally plucked up the courage to climb through the fence and stood on the other side, swishing his torch to and fro. The woods were as dark as the inside of a cave – if not darker. Cravins Creek Forest was an eerie place to be at night. Even though Charlie was brave and intrepid, it didn't stop his knees knocking. Thankfully, he didn't have too far to go to meet Whizzy, for their secret place was close to the edge of the forest.

'This better be important, Whizzy, dragging me out at night...' he muttered to himself.

Charlie didn't hang about. He ran between the mighty trees, his torch beam pinballing from tree trunk to tree trunk in search for the secret marker he was looking for, until he eventually came upon it. It was carved into an enormous redwood tree. The carving was of an owl, no bigger than the palm of his hand. It pointed to their secret hideout.

Charlie had arrived.

He shone his torch up the mighty tree trunk to where, nestled discreetly thirty feet up, was their treehouse. For many years it had remained unnoticed by passers-by. Even the forest rangers didn't know it existed; either that or they turned a blind eye to it, as no construction of any kind was allowed in the forest.

To keep it protected from intruders, the only way to access the treehouse was by scaling a tall tree nearby and climbing over, which was no easy feat, even for experienced climbers – or access could be gained if someone was in the treehouse and lowered a rope ladder to the ground.

Charlie hoped that Whizzy had already arrived. There was only one way to find out. He cupped his hands and blew into them, imitating an owl's hoot. This was their signal. When there was no reply, he wondered if perhaps Whizzy had not heard him, so he tried once more. But that attempt also met with silence.

To save himself from further embarrassment – his attempt to sound like an owl had sounded more like the calling of a cheeky chimpanzee – Charlie hissed, loud enough for his friend to hear, 'Psst! Whizzy, it's Charlie. Drop down the rope ladder, would you?'

But nothing happened. Whizzy clearly hadn't arrived yet. This meant Charlie had to climb up to the treehouse in the dark, something he was not happy about at all.

Charlie climbed up carefully, like Jack climbing the beanstalk. At the top, he clung to the tree, choosing big branches as he made his way over to their tree. By the time he reached the treehouse he was exhausted, and barely had the energy to heave himself up over the rail. Then a shadowy figure with an enormous head came charging out from the doorway towards him, howling and growling, and holding a weapon of some kind.

When Charlie saw this, he let out a terrified yell and accidentally let go of the support rail. As he was falling, the big-headed thing quickly reached out and grabbed Charlie's hoodie.

'Got you!' said a voice.

The thing pulled Charlie back in. He clung to the rails for dear life, staring in horror at the person. It took him a second to figure out who it was, and when he did his face turned to thunder. He shone the torch at the other person and said angrily, 'What the hell are you playing at, Whizzy? You scared the living daylights out of me, charging at me like that!' Charlie climbed over the rail. 'Never mind the fact that I nearly fell because of you!'

'Sorry, Charlie, I didn't know it was you!' Whizzy sounded apologetic.

'Haven't you got your torch with you?' Charlie questioned.

'I dropped it when I was climbing up. It's down there somewhere,' replied Whizzy.

'Well, didn't you hearing me calling up to you?'

Whizzy shook his head.

'Well, perhaps if you didn't have that stupid thing on your head then you might – wait a second, why are you wearing a hockey helmet? Isn't that your sister's boyfriend's helmet?' Charlie looked oddly at Whizzy.

'To protect myself, in case they come for us out here,' Whizzy said, picking up a hockey stick.

Charlie felt unsettled by his words. 'In case who comes for us? Whizzy, you're not making any sense. Why are we out here?'

'Can we please go inside? I'll explain there. It gives me the creeps out here.'

Charlie could see Whizzy was really troubled by whatever it was he had to tell him. He simply nodded in agreement and followed him through the doorway.

It was pitch black inside the treehouse, and unusually cold. The boys fumbled around and located a box of matches in an old tin in the corner of the room. Charlie went around lighting the lanterns. Once they were all lit, the treehouse glowed charmingly. The room was decorated in an array of colours. The panelled walls were strong and sturdy. In the centre of the room, the tree trunk soared up through the floor and through the wooden roof, which had sections etched out as handholds. Logs had been chopped down to size and made into stools, and drawings, paintings, dreamcatchers and photos of the children hung about the place, while some toys and games lay dotted across the floor.

'Eww, how long's it been since we came up here?' Charlie said, wiping away a huge cobweb that he'd walked into.

'It's been a while,' Whizzy replied, 'but it was the safest place I could come up with for us to meet.'

'Alright, Whizzy, spit it out. What's going on? What do you have to tell me?' Charlie demanded, placing his hands on his hips.

Whizzy removed his helmet and set it down on the floor. He put his glasses back on, pulled an envelope out of his pocket and handed it to Charlie.

'What's this?' Charlie said, looking baffled.

'The reason we're out here,' Whizzy said, sighing.

Charlie unfolded the envelope and slid the note out. The second he read it, he felt as if his heart had stopped. He looked at Whizzy with an expression of shock and disbelief.

'Is this some kind of joke? Because if it is...' he began.

'Would I joke about something this serious?' Whizzy said bluntly. 'Those masked people have kidnapped Bridget! What are we going to do?'

When he heard Whizzy say the words, Charlie felt as if he had been punched in the stomach. He read the lines over and over again, hoping to find a mistake or an error. Perhaps he had read it wrong?

But he hadn't. It was printed there in black and white:

> You have something of ours. It doesn't belong to you. Bring it to Baverslocke Airfield in Little Valley tomorrow night at 10 p.m.
>
> A word of warning: don't tell anyone, including the police. We have your friend Bridget and we will kill her if you tell anyone.
>
> Bring us the Blue Star and we will release your friend. Don't, and she dies!

Charlie felt an overwhelming fear. He looked at Whizzy and stuttered, 'No, no, this can't be true! Where did you get this?'

Whizzy gulped and wrung his hands as he stared at Charlie, looking guilty.

'Whizzy?'

Silence.

'Answer me, Whizzy!' Charlie shouted.

Whizzy flinched, then responded in a quiet voice, 'Well, after you guys left, I thought I'd have another go at hacking Amspatrax's system, see if I could find out anything else about Salvador. I was almost in, but then my computer died on me. Then I heard the floorboards creak above my head. I thought it was Jadanna, because she'd been home once already to check on me and had gone back out again. Then there was a bang from upstairs, so I went to check it out.

'Then someone came up behind me and grabbed me. I almost died! But when I turned around, I saw it was Mom. She and Dad had got back early from visiting my aunt out of town.

'I followed my rents into the kitchen for a quick chat. Mom saw the back door was open and went mad, because the last time I accidentally left it open, a raccoon came wandering in and ate her freshly baked pie. But I thought it was weird that it was open, because I knew I'd closed it after seeing you guys out. I knew it wasn't Jadanna as she always uses the front door, never the back.

'Anyway, as I was leaving the kitchen, Mom said there was a letter for me on the counter. As soon as I saw what it said, I just stood there, frozen. Mom asked me if I was alright, but I didn't say anything. I just went straight to my room. I didn't know what to do. For a long time, I sat there, staring at my computer, wondering what I'd done. Amspatrax must've found out where I lived the first time

I hacked into its website and sent men to come and find me. Now I know why my computer died – those good-for-nothing jerks reverse-hacked it and crashed it. I don't know if I can repair it.' He sighed.

Charlie felt devastated that Bridget had been kidnapped, and a deep sense of guilt was eating away at him. In a fit of rage, he picked up the log beside him and threw it across the room. The wall panelling cracked and split where the log hit it.

'I COULDN'T GIVE A MONKEY'S ABOUT YOUR STUPID COMPUTER!' he screamed.

Whizzy jumped in fright.

'Don't you get it? Our best friend's been taken hostage by Salvador and all you care about is your stupid computer!'

'That's not true,' Whizzy protested. 'Of course I care. I was in shock when I got that note.'

Eventually, Charlie slumped to the floor. 'This is all my fault. Bridget was right. I should have never taken the crystal. I'm such a darn fool.'

Whizzy came over and placed his hand sympathetically upon his shoulder. 'Look, I'm just as much to blame for this as you are. If I hadn't hacked into their system, thinking I was so clever, they probably would never have found us.' He bowed his head.

Charlie wiped his nose with his arm and turned to look at Whizzy. 'We have to get her back, Whizzy. Whatever it takes, we have to get our friend back. I'll never forgive myself if anything happens to her.'

'But how?' asked Whizzy. 'You read what it said: if we don't give them back the Blue Star tomorrow night, they'll kill her!'

Charlie couldn't think straight. His mind was clouded with worry. But then something came to him from out of the blue. He jumped to his feet.

'Where are you going?' Whizzy said, looking confused at Charlie's impulsive behaviour. Whizzy got up and followed him out onto the balcony. 'Charlie, where are you going? We need to talk this over.'

Charlie didn't respond. He pulled a lever and a trapdoor in the floor fell open, releasing the rope ladder. He climbed down onto the wooden steps and stopped to look back at Whizzy, his head just above the level of the floor. 'I need to check something. You coming?'

'You don't have to ask me twice – I ain't staying here by myself,' Whizzy replied, and ran back inside to blow out the lanterns before mounting the ladder himself.

Once the boys had reached the ground, Charlie tugged on a handle attached to a dangling piece of rope beside the tree. This sent the rope ladder back up to the treehouse, along with the rope: a nice piece of ingenuity on Whizzy's part. He had come up with the design. The boys ran back through the forest, heading in the direction of the main road, slid through the broken fence and ran up their street, passing Charlie's house along the way. As always, Whizzy did his best to keep up with Charlie, who ran like a cheetah. Charlie came to a grinding halt outside one of the houses in the street.

'It was here!' he said breathlessly, pacing back and forth while staring up and down the road. 'It was right here!'

'What was here?' Whizzy said, wiping sweat away from his forehead.

'The van with the blacked-out windows I saw earlier. It was parked right here, outside Mrs Coleman's house. I clocked it when I was walking back with Bridget after leaving yours. I knew there wasn't something right when I saw it. Damn it!' Angrily, he punched his hand into his palm.

'Well, it's not here now,' Whizzy said, gasping, 'so what do we do now?'

Charlie's mouth opened as if he was about to say something, when flashing blue lights in the distance caught his attention. It was a police car, and it was heading towards them at a considerable rate. Thinking it was coming for them, Charlie grabbed Whizzy by the arm and pulled him behind a parked car. The pair ducked down out of sight. When the police vehicle blew past them, they sighed with relief. But Charlie had a feeling he knew where it was heading. He looked at Whizzy and they said simultaneously, 'Bridget's.'

The pair chased the police car. They took a shortcut down a side street, ran down a back alleyway, crossed over into Miderson Ave, cut through a small section of the forest and ran up the narrow lane that led to Bridget's house. By the time they got there, behind the private gates of the estate they saw the police car parked in Bridget's driveway, as they had expected.

The boys hid behind a tree and watched nervously as the police chief got out of the car and walked up to the door, where Bridget's dad, Mike, stood, consoling Bridget's mom, Sarah. The three of them went inside.

'On second thoughts, perhaps we should tell the police what's happened to her,' Whizzy said, turning to Charlie.

'And risk our best friend being killed? Have you lost your mind? No way, Whizzy, this is our mess and we need to sort it out ourselves. It's up to us to get Bridget back,' Charlie said adamantly. 'C'mon, we better head off before our parents find us gone and report us missing.' And off they sprinted back up the lane.

CHAPTER 7

OFFICER GOOFBALL

The next morning, Charlie trudged down the green-carpeted stairs, looking miserable. He'd hardly got any sleep. He'd tossed and turned all night, cold sweat bathing his body, dreaming about his best friend being taken. He felt sick. The burden of guilt weighed heavily upon him, so much so that he decided he'd tell his mom everything at breakfast.

But Charlie changed his mind the moment he turned into the living room, rubbing his tired eyes. There he saw something that stopped him dead in his tracks. In the middle of the room were three people, two of whom were engaged in a serious conversation, by the look on their faces. One of them was Charlie's mom, Debby, who stopped speaking the second he entered.

'Charlie!' Debby said in surprise.

Charlie felt his stomach drop.

He glanced away from his mom at the other person she'd been speaking to, and dread filled him. The stout man standing beside Charlie's mom was familiar. He was the police chief, Stanley Causeway. But Charlie didn't recognise the other police officer. He stood behind Chief Causeway, leaning against the wooden mantelpiece, his hands casually resting on his duty belt, rolling his tongue over his shiny gold tooth.

The young officer must've been new to the police department in Cravins Creek, Charlie presumed. He took an instant dislike to him. He was thin and lanky with cropped black hair, sporting a handlebar moustache that looked as if it'd been stuck on for a fancy-dress party, and he had a squint in one eye. His uniform was far too big for him – it looked like he'd borrowed it from Chief Causeway.

A proper goofball, Charlie thought to himself.

Debby smiled sadly at Charlie – the kind of smile that suggested something bad had happened, and any second now she was about to break terrible news to him. He remembered her wearing the same expression when she told him that his dad had died. But this time it wasn't about his dad, nor was his mom tearing up, and Charlie already knew what the problem was. It had kept him awake all night.

'Hey, slugger,' Chief Causeway said, acknowledging him with a jerk of his head and a gentle smile. 'How's that swing of yours coming along?'

Charlie's eye briefly met Chief Causeway's. 'Good, thanks, Stan,' he muttered before quickly looking back to his mom.

'Morning, sweetie, did you sleep okay?' said Debby.

Charlie nodded. 'What's going on, Mom? Is everything alright?' he said, trying to remain calm.

Debby cleared her throat and held her hand to her chest. 'Well, the reason Stan's here, Charlie, with...' She paused.

'Officer Balecoomb, ma'am,' said the young police officer, giving an irritating smirk and managing to look like a sly fox.

'Yes, Officer Balecoomb,' said Debby, flushing. 'Well, the reason they've come is because there's a problem.'

Charlie's felt his hands turn clammy with sweat. He could see his mom was struggling to speak.

'What kind of problem?' he said, looking concerned.

'Why don't you come take a seat, sweetie, so I can explain,' Debby said softly.

'What's the problem, Mom? Is Evan alright?' he said.

'Yes.'

'Then what is it?' Charlie said, leaning against her.

Before Debby had chance to tell her son the issue, Chief Causeway interceded and said in a gruff voice, 'The problem is, one of your friends has gone missing.'

Charlie felt his heart skip a beat.

'W-w-what? Who?' he stammered, looking at Chief Causeway and his mother with genuine worry.

Debby looked sad. 'It's Bridget, baby. She's disappeared yesterday.'

Hearing her name, Charlie felt a crushing pain in his heart. His eyes started to brim with tears. Immediately his mother moved to console him and held him tightly; a good job she did, as he wasn't sure how much longer he could keep up the pretence without confessing to what he really knew.

'Oh, sweetie,' said Debby, kissing him on the top of his head.

Charlie felt rotten to the core. He loved his mom dearly and hated having to lie to her, but what choice did he have? These people had threatened to kill his best friend if Charlie and Whizzy went blabbering to anyone. However, while he stood there hugging his mom, he sensed someone's eyes burning a hole in the back of his head.

Out of the corner of his eye he could see Officer Balecoomb eyeballing him, so he buried his head in his mother's chest. Debby smiled at him.

'I know this is upsetting for you to hear, baby, and I'm sure there's a perfectly reasonable explanation for why this has happened. But right now, baby, the police have a job to do. They want to find Bridget as quickly as they can and bring her home safe and well to her parents, so they've come to ask you a few questions about her. Is that okay?' asked Debby.

Charlie nodded. His mom led him over to the old sofa, where they took a seat and he held her warm hand.

Chief Causeway dragged a chair across the wooden dining-room floor, scuffing up the rug in the process. He positioned the chair in front of the pair before dumping his heavy bottom down on it. He removed his hat and placed it on the coffee table, then brushed his sausage fingers through his receding silvery brown hair. He looked raddled and unkempt; his uniformed was creased, as if he'd slept in it, and he stank of cigarettes and coffee. Even from a few feet away, Charlie could smell him. After twenty-nine years of serving as the town's police chief, he looked tired. He cleared his throat.

'As your mother said, Charlie, we want to find Bridget as quickly as possible and bring her safely home, so if there's anything you can tell us, no matter how small, then please do.'

Charlie glanced at Officer Balecoomb, who was still watching him like a hawk. Charlie dismissed him and went back to looking sorrowfully at Chief Causeway. 'What do you want to know?' he asked, sniffing.

The chair creaked under Chief Causeway's weight as he leaned forward to rest his thick forearms on his legs. The buttons on his shirt looked as if they were about to pop off under the pressure of his bulging belly.

'Well, how 'bout you start by telling me when was the last time you saw Bridget?' Chief Causeway said, giving Charlie a friendly smile.

Charlie told the chief what he and his friends had been up to the day before, but deliberately left out what they had discovered in the forest. Chief Causeway leaned back in the chair, his expression thoughtful, his baggy eyes narrowing. 'You say you and your friends were playing in the forest yesterday?'

Charlie nodded.

'You didn't by any chance see anything unusual while you were playing there?' Chief Causeway said.

'Like what?' Charlie said timidly.

Chief Causeway's lips parted to speak, when Office Balecoomb interrupted.

'Like a plane, kid,' he drawled.

Charlie felt a sinking feeling in his stomach. He darted a look at Officer Balecoomb. Damn, they know about the plane. That's bad, he thought. If the police know about the wreckage, surely they'll know about everything else...

'A plane?' Debby said in a shocked tone. Her timing was perfect to deflect the scrutiny Charlie felt under.

'That's right, ma'am.'

'Why on earth would there be a plane in Cravins Creek Forest?' Debby queried, glancing at the men.

'We're not sure,' Chief Causeway said quickly, glaring furiously at Officer Balecoomb as if to stop him saying any more, 'but we're looking into it to find out what happened.'

Debby eyed Chief Causeway and Officer Balecoomb suspiciously. 'I see.'

Chief Causeway turned his attention back to Charlie, who shifted uncomfortably.

'So you say you saw nothing while you were in the forest, Charlie?' he said.

Charlie shook his head.

'And after you finished playing in the forest, you say the three of you went to Cody's house. How long would you say you were there for?' Chief Causeway asked.

'Dunno. A couple of hours, I guess,' Charlie said, thinking back.

'And when you and Bridget left Cody's house, you say you both went straight home?' Chief Causeway said.

'Yeah,' replied Charlie. 'I was hungry, and Skyla needed feeding, so...'

'And you didn't go anywhere else after leaving Cody's?'

'No,' Charlie said, shaking his head vehemently. 'I came straight home, like I said.'

'And as far as you know, Bridget went home as well?'

'Yeah.'

'Did you see anyone suspicious around?'

Charlie broke eye contact with Chief Causeway for a second. The black van.

'Are you okay, sweetie?' he heard his mom say.

'No,' Charlie answered quietly, looking down.

'Did Bridget say anything to you about being unhappy, or—'

'Okay, I think that's enough questions for today, Stan,' Debby intervened.

'It's okay, Mom, I don't mind answering,' said Charlie, turning to her then looking Chief Causeway in the eye. 'Bridget was Bridget; she was always happy around us. If she ever had a problem, she would tell us. We don't keep secrets from each other.'

Chief Causeway smiled. 'Well, I think we're about done here, Thanks for your time. We'll be in touch.' He got up.

Charlie bolted to his feet. 'You will find Bridget, Chief, won't you?' he said pleadingly.

'We'll do our best, Charlie, but in the meantime, if you hear anything, be sure to let us know, won't you?' Chief Causeway put on his hat.

'See you again, kid,' Officer Balecoomb said smugly.

Debby saw the men to the door and said to Chief Causeway, 'Hey, Stan, can I have a word?'

'Give us a minute, would you?' Chief Causeway said, jerking his head to Officer Balecoomb, who stepped outside and shut the door.

Charlie could hear them talking quietly, and moved over to the wall to eavesdrop on their conversation.

'I see you got yourself a rookie, Officer Balecoomb.' Debby giggled.

Chief Causeway shook his head despairingly. 'The lad's gotta lot to learn.'

'He doesn't seem all that bad,' Debby said. 'Could be worse. Could be like the last one they sent you.'

Chief Causeway chortled. 'Don't wish that on me, will you?'

'So, what do you think's happened to Bridget? Her parents must be worried sick about her,' Debby said, folding her arms.

'Hard to say at this point.' The chief shrugged. 'I know Sarah and Mike have been having some problems at home recently. We could be dealing with a runaway.'

'Are you sure? I wouldn't think Bridget was the type to run away. She's such a sweet little girl.'

'Who knows what goes on behind closed doors?' replied Chief Causeway. 'You only gotta look at the Sasmia's to know the troubles their family have gone through.'

'True,' Debby said, raising her eyebrows. 'God, I wish they'd tear that hideous house down or sell it or do something with it, it's such a sight. So, what's this about finding a plane in the forest?'

'It's classified information while it's still under investigation,' Chief Causeway said firmly.

'Classified, my backside, Stan,' Debby said, placing her hands on her hips. 'When has that stopped you before?'

Chief Causeway stood there, tight-lipped.

'Fine. I'll find out from Betty when I meet with her on Tuesday. I'm sure she won't be too pleased when I let slip to her that you came to pay me a visit smelling of cigarettes. I was under the impression you'd given up, on the doctor's advice?'

Chief Causeway sniffed his shirt and rolled his eyes. 'It was only one, maybe two,' he said guiltily.

'Tell that to Betty when she finds out,' Debby said, smirking.

'That's cold. Y'know, I could have you arrested for blackmailing an officer of the law.'

Debby held her hands out. Chief Causeway shook his head disapprovingly. 'You're as ballsy as your father, God rest his good soul. Alright, here's the thing: this goes no further, do you hear me? I received a call yesterday from the forest rangers to say that, while they were out patrolling, they came across the remains of a cockpit from a plane that had crashed in the forest.'

'Were there any survivors?' Debby asked.

'We've found one body so far. The pilot. He was found dead in the cockpit,' said Chief Causeway.

'Gosh,' said Debby, 'so do you have any idea how it got there?'

'Not yet,' Chief Causeway said, shaking his head. 'The patrol boys are still out looking for the rest of the plane, but I'll say this to you, Debs. Keep an eye on Charlie and make sure he doesn't go anywhere near the forest while this investigation is going on.'

'Will do,' replied Debby.

'On that note, I'm off. I have to go and pay the Carters a visit regarding Bridget's disappearance.' Chief Causeway opened the front door, stepped out and turned to Debby. 'Be sure to say hello to Evan for me, and when you see Betty, zip it – or else.'

Debby nodded with a smile.

Charlie heard the door close and darted off to his room. From his window he saw Chief Causeway stop halfway up the drive, ranting at Officer Balecoomb about something, but he couldn't hear what. After he'd finished, he walked away along the street, leaving the young officer standing there. Officer Balecoomb trotted to catch him up, and they strolled towards Whizzy's house.

Charlie frantically searched his room for his walkie-talkie, as he couldn't remember where he'd put it the night before, and found it underneath his pillow.

'Slugger to Whizzy, Slugger to Whizzy, do you read me, over!' he repeated over and over.

Eventually a tired voice answered his call. 'Whizzy here. Whasupp? Over.'

'The police are on their way to your house. I repeat, the police are on their way to your house. Over!' Charlie cried.

'WHAT? What do you mean, the police are on their way here? Oh dear lord, they've found out, haven't they? They know I hacked into Amspatrax and now they're coming to arrest me and throw me in jail!' Whizzy said, panicking.

'Whizzy, calm down, would you?' Charlie yelled. 'No one's coming to arrest you!'

'Oh. So why are they coming here?'

'For a smart person, you really are dumb sometimes. Because of Bridget!'

'Have they found her?' Whizzy asked.

'No, nothing has changed since last night,' Charlie said, sounding frustrated. 'Listen, would you, 'cause we haven't got long to talk. Any second now they'll be knocking on your door and wanting to speak to you and you won't know what to say.' Charlie peered out at the street.

Charlie told Whizzy about the conversation he'd had with the police and prompted him on what to say so they said the same thing. It was risky, but Charlie had to be sure that Whizzy was well informed. Charlie knew how nervous Whizzy got.

'Now, don't forget what I told you. If you do, and you mess this up by saying the wrong thing, you're gonna land us both in big trouble. Got it?'

'Got it,' replied Whizzy.

'Oh, and one other thing. Remember, lots of tears!' said Charlie.

'Hey...'

'What?' Charlie said irritably.

'Well, you still haven't said how we're gonna get Bridget back,' Whizzy said.

'Never mind that,' Charlie said dismissively. 'Right now I need you to focus on what you're going to say to Chief Causeway and Officer Goofball – but don't call him that, whatever you do. And one last thing: make sure you hit me back the second they're gone.'

'Affirmative – oh, they're here. Gotta go!' The radio went dead.

Charlie puffed out his cheeks, put the walkie-talkie down on the windowsill, and threw himself down onto his bed. He stared despairingly at the ceiling, praying that Whizzy wouldn't blow it and spill the beans to the police. He couldn't believe he'd managed to hold his nerve when questioned by them himself. He knew that lying to the police was a terrible thing to do. He felt ashamed. Then again, the cause was justified, he reminded himself. He didn't think that Officer Goofball had been convinced by what he had said, but as long as Chief Causeway kept him in check it would be okay.

There came a knock on his bedroom door, and his mom appeared.

'Hey sweetie, can I come in?' Debby asked.

Charlie bolted upright and nodded glumly.

Debby sat down beside him on the bed and placed her hands on top of his. 'Aw, baby, I know this must be real hard for you, but I'm sure Chief Causeway will do everything in his power to find Bridget and bring her back safe and well.'

Charlie found no comfort in his mother's words. He stared despondently at the floor.

'I tell you what. Why don't you come downstairs with me and I'll fix you some of your favourite maple syrup pancakes for breakfast. How does that sound?' Debby suggested, smiling affectionately at him.

The thought of eating his favourite pancakes right now turned his stomach. Charlie stared into his mom's caring green eyes.

'Thanks,' he replied, 'but I kind of want to be left alone right now.'

Debby sighed. 'Listen to me, Charlie. If there's anything on your mind, you know you can tell me, don't you? Don't keep it bottled up inside.'

Words of confession were on the verge of tumbling right out of Charlie's mouth. He had to work hard not to tell his mom the truth. He nodded unhappily.

Debby stroked his hair before giving him a kiss on his forehead, then left the room.

Charlie heaved a sigh and fell back down onto the bed again. He turned his head to stare at the alarm clock. It was almost ten o'clock. In twelve hours' time he needed to be at Baverslocke Airfield with the crystal, or else. It was an abandoned airfield that had previously been used as a flying school by two military veterans: Tom Bavers and Jeremy Locke. It was five miles north of Cravins Creek in Little Valley, the neighbouring town.

What was he going to do? How were he and Whizzy going to rescue Bridget? He didn't have the faintest notion. All he knew was that these men must want the Blue Star *really* badly if they were prepared to kidnap a young girl and take her hostage for it. These were real dangerous people he was dealing with here.

He heard his bedroom door creak, and swivelled his head. It was Skyla. She came wandering in, licking her lips, and jumped onto the bed beside him. She rested her head on his chest while Charlie stroked her soft fur.

'Oh Skyla, what a mess I'm in. What am I going to do?' he said to her. Skyla gave him a friendly lick on his chin.

Charlie closed his eyes. He didn't realise he had drifted off to sleep until, sometime later, the radio woke him, hissing and crackling. He leapt out of bed and raced over to the window.

It was Whizzy, requesting that they rendezvous at the park at twelve hundred hours.

CHAPTER 8

RACE AGAINST TIME

Charlie looked at his watch for the umpteenth time. It was 9.36 p.m. Whizzy was now very late. Charlie had been waiting impatiently for him on his BMX under a streetlight, shadowed by the trees.

'Where the fricking 'ell is he?' he fumed, staring vacantly up the road.

The boys had arranged to meet on the corner of West Mont Avenue and Burgess Road at 9.15 p.m., but for some reason, Whizzy hadn't shown. This wasn't a good sign. In fact, it was disastrous. For the plan Charlie had come up with earlier in the treehouse relied on Whizzy. Without him, it wasn't going to work. Had Whizzy let Charlie know he wasn't going to come, then perhaps Charlie might have had time to come up with a Plan B. But Whizzy wasn't even responding to Charlie's calls on the walkie-talkie.

Charlie couldn't wait any longer. The ride out to Baverslocke Airfield would take the best part of thirty minutes and, thanks to Whizzy, Charlie was behind schedule.

'Frigging yellow-belly. I knew he wouldn't go through with it,' Charlie growled, kicking his pedal around aggressively to push off. As he cycled down the road, he heard a faint cry.

'Charlie, CHARLIE!'

Charlie abruptly stopped his bike and looked back over his shoulder. Overwhelming relief filled him to see his buddy pedalling like a lunatic up the road. Whizzy hand-braked his bike, skidding it sideways beside Charlie. He was red in the face and out of breath.

'Bud, where the blazes have you been? I thought you'd chickened out! I was just about to leave without you!' Charlie said.

'I got held up by Mom coming into my room. Long story. I'll explain later,' Whizzy said, draping himself over his handlebars, 'but thanks for waiting for me.'

'Did you bring it with you?' Charlie asked, looking concerned.

Whizzy patted the side of his backpack. 'Right here,' he said.

Charlie beamed with delight. 'Excellent! Now c'mon, let's go get our friend back!' They gave each other a high-five and set off up the road.

*

The main road leading north out of town was dark, windy, and creepy as a graveyard to travel along at night. There were no streetlights to light the way. Since the road cut through the heart of Cravins Creek Forest, it was well known for the presence of black bears and other wild animals that weren't usually seen by day. Charlie planned on taking the west road, had they set off early enough; a longer route, but one that was less intimidating and far better lit. But like it or not, this was the quickest way to get to Baverslocke Airfield.

In every direction the boys turned, forbidding darkness surrounded them. It felt as if there was no end in sight. The only light was their bike lights, illuminating the road ahead. The boys rode close together, side by side, feeling the cold wind rush against their faces as fear drove them to pedal as fast as they could.

The boys freewheeled down an exceptionally long hill. The moment they came out of it and straightened up, Charlie saw a pair of eyes glinting in the middle of the road up ahead.

'Whizzy, look out!' Charlie yelled.

The pair were travelling too fast to stop. At the last second, they swerved around the wolf, one on either side. The wolf snapped its jaws as they flew past, but did not chase the boys.

'Woohoo, did you see that?' Charlie said, feeling a rush of excitement. Whizzy looked scared half to death. 'That wolf took a swipe at us! Good job it was too occupied munching whatever it was munching to come chasing after us.'

'Thank goodness,' Whizzy replied in a trembling voice. 'I don't fancy being mauled to death by a wolf.'

Before long the ominous forest came to an end, much to their relief. Beyond, the road snaked through the prairie, reaching out into the distance and touching the moonlit sky.

'Jeez, I don't recall the airfield being this far out, Charlie,' Whizzy groaned.

'That's because we ain't been out here for yonks,' Charlie said between breaths. 'It shouldn't be much further now.'

The boys pedalled on into the night, finally reaching a crossroads. There, a sign pointed in the direction of Little Valley, which pleased them. It was another five or so miles to the town itself, though, luckily, they weren't heading that far. The boys took a sharp left, skidding around the corner. By now, sweat was pouring down Charlie's face and his legs were burning. But he didn't care. The thought of reaching his friend on time spurred him on and he rode harder than ever.

Half a mile up the road, the pair passed a sign saying 'Welcome to Little Valley'. Shortly after that, Charlie suddenly cranked his right knee out, as did Whizzy, and the pair joined a dirt track, leaving the main road behind them. They bounced along it as if they were riding down a flight of steps. They rode in single file along a narrow track leading through a coppice until it eventually brought them out onto an open plain. The boys jammed on their brakes, leaving tyre marks on the moist ground, and brought their bikes to a grinding halt. They switched their lights off and sat in the silent field, panting, gazing at the derelict airfield buildings.

Charlie checked his watch. It was 9.56 p.m. 'We made it with a couple of minutes to spare!'

'It looks like there's no one's here, Charlie,' said Whizzy.

'No, it doesn't,' said Charlie. 'I bet my bottom dollar they're here somewhere waiting for us. Well, there's no point standing around here.'

'You're not seriously considering going in there, are you? Not after what happened last time, when that maniac started chasing us and I almost fell through the floor?' Fear filled Whizzy's eyes.

'He wasn't a maniac.' Charlie chortled. 'He was just a hobo. Besides, you needn't worry. You're staying out here with the crystal, like we planned.'

'You sure this is gonna to work, Charlie? Maybe I should come in there with you,' Whizzy stammered, staring around the dark field.

Charlie felt as doubtful as Whizzy sounded. His stomach was tied up in knots. But he wasn't going to let it show, certainly not to Whizzy. His best friends always looked up to him and he always tried to act courageously in front of them, though admittedly on this occasion he wasn't feeling so confident.

'Trust me, it'll work, just as long as we stick to the plan. Speaking of which, let's run through it one more time so we know exactly what we're doing. Alright, so when I'm off looking for them, where're you gonna be?' Charlie said.

'Here, on standby, waiting to receive your instructions,' Whizzy said.

'Good. And while I'm in there demanding they release Bridget before we hand over the crystal, I'm gonna need you to be ready with your walkie-talkie in case any of these guys tries any funny business. You got your walkie-talkie with you?' Charlie said, pointing at him.

Whizzy pulled the radio out of the side pocket of his backpack and held it up. 'Check.'

'Great.'

'Wait a second, Charlie, just run through what happens if they refuse to release Bridget unless you give them the Blue Star first?' Whizzy said.

'If that happens, then I'll hit you up on the radio and say' – Charlie held his radio to his mouth and pretended to do a run-through – '"Slugger to Whizzy, are you ready to go to the police, over?", then you say, "Whizzy to Slugger, I'm ready to go to them, over" then when they realise we're serious and we ain't messing around, they'll have no choice but to release Bridget first. But remember, Whizzy, if you haven't heard from me or seen me leave with Bridget within the next fifteen minutes, I want you to ride as fast as you can to Little Valley and go straight to the police department with the crystal and tell them everything you know. Got it?'

'Got it,' Whizzy said, an undertone of nervousness in his voice.

Charlie looked at his watch again. It was 9.57 p.m. He turned to Whizzy, who looked frightened, and tried to reassure him. 'Hey, it'll be fine, we got this.' He clapped him on the shoulder.

Whizzy gave an unconvincing nod. They performed their pack handshake, then hugged each other.

'Remember, Whizzy, fifteen minutes: if you don't hear me or see from me, you go straight to the police and tell them everything.'

'Fifteen minutes,' Whizzy repeated.

Charlie was about to take off across the field when Whizzy grabbed him by the arm and stopped him. 'Hey, Charlie, just be sure to bring our friend back with you.'

Charlie nodded grimly.

Whizzy watched Charlie ride off into the darkness until he could no longer see him, after which he stood there, shaking like a leaf. Creepy night-time noises surrounded him. He hadn't been there long when a clap of thunder ruptured the sky, making him jump almost as high as the moon. Whizzy jerked his head upward to see the cloudless night sky filled with glistening stars, and quietly began counting to himself, applying the flash-to-bang rule to see how far away the storm was. After counting for what felt like ages, a perplexed look fell over his face.

'That's weird,' he muttered. 'There was no flash.'

Then from nowhere a bizarre noise emerged, a sound that started off as a low enigmatic rumble and grew louder. Whizzy searched the landscape as far as he could see, but he couldn't see where the noise was coming from.

Then a huge gust of wind came blasting down from the sky and almost flattened him. Whizzy swung back around, tilted his head back and stared into the deep black sky.

His eyebrows rose and his eyes grew round. He couldn't believe what he saw. The sky rippled, and the outline of something enormous appeared. There was no denying what it was. Whizzy dropped his walkie-talkie in shock. It was a spaceship, and it was slowly gliding towards the huge administrative building where Charlie had headed.

CHAPTER 9

UNEXPECTED VISITORS

Meanwhile, Charlie had left his BMX leaning against the brick wall of the building and had already ventured inside. It was pitch dark – just as well he had remembered to bring his torch. It was stowed inside his backpack. Swishing it to and fro, he nervously took tentative steps along a long corridor. His feet crunched over something on the ground – stones? Gravel? The airfield had been abandoned for decades and, over time, it had seen its fair share of vandals pass through. The concrete walls were smeared in graffiti, and the place stank like a sewer.

Charlie held his breath.

He walked on, filled with trepidation, to the end of the corridor. He could only go left. On he continued, stepping in small puddles of stagnant water, then through a set of double doors that had been torn from their hinges. Further ahead was a steel door. The sound of the metal scraping across the stone floor sent shivers up his spine as he heaved it open. Then the corridor ended and Charlie was in a vast open space. Before he could go any further, the unexpected happened: the light from his torch began to dim.

'No, no, no!' he said, panicking and shaking the torch forcefully.

The light grew brighter for long enough for him to spot something out of the ordinary. He panned the light back to it. It was the shiny chrome front grille of a vehicle.

'That's weird,' he mumbled to himself. 'Why is there—'

Before Charlie had a chance to think anything else, its headlights lit up, followed by two others. Dazzled, Charlie lurched away. When he opened his eyes, he saw, to his dismay, multiple beams of red light, as thin as wire, all aimed at him.

'Don't move!' a voice yelled from somewhere in the darkness.

Charlie had no intention of moving. He stood there, startled, his heart racing.

Then there was the sound of a vehicle door opening and closing. It echoed in the darkness. Then there were heavy footsteps. The footsteps stopped in front of the middle vehicle, so its headlights cast a silhouette of a tall shadowy figure.

'Glad to see you made it, Charles ... Theodore ... Sprewell.'

Charlie recognised the man's distinctive silky-smooth voice. It was Enoch Salvador. But how did he know his name?

'Do you know who I am?' Salvador asked.

Charlie held his hand up to shield his eyes, and squinted through his fingers. 'I-I know who you are.' His voice broke. 'You're the douchebag who took my friend.'

'Well, it wasn't me personally,' Salvador said with a malignant laugh, 'and for good reason. Now tell me, what else do you know, Charles?'

Charlie hesitated, considering the question. 'Nothing. All I'm here for is to get my friend back.'

'I find that hard to believe, since your other little buddy, who I don't see here, has proved himself to be quite the genius. Hacking into my company's systems – it's never been done before, you know. Though my team of experts were soon able to trace his location. Not as smart as he thinks he is. And, speaking of the little parasite, where is he?'

Charlie felt himself tremble inside, but now was not the time to let it show. He plucked up all his courage and said in a brave voice, 'Never mind him. Where's my friend Bridget? What have you done with her?'

'Well, let's just say she's a little tied up.' Salvador gave a contemptuous laugh. 'But she's safe and in perfectly good hands, so you needn't worry. Now, I believe you took something of mine, and you've come here to return it?'

Charlie shook his head. 'Not before I see my friend,' he said daringly.

There was a pause, then the sound of Salvador's footsteps crunching on the gravelly ground. He walked slowly towards Charlie.

'Did you know, Charles, long before you were born, or even I for that matter, this airfield was used by the government as a military base during World War Two? Ironic – the very government I despise using this for their expendable military, but if there's one thing I loathe more than our government, it's a recalcitrant child.'

Charlie tipped his head back to stare at the stone-faced, black-suited slender man who towered over him. His aftershave reminded Charlie of vinegar; it was horrid.

'Why don't you be a good little boy and hand me the Blue Star? Then we can forget all about this misunderstanding and you and your friend Bridget can run along back to the rock you crawled out from,' Salvador said, holding his hand out.

Charlie took a defiant step back, causing all the red dots to shift about erratically on his chest. 'You'll never get your hands on the crystal, Salvador, because I've hidden it, and I won't tell you where it is unless I see my friend first!'

Salvador's jaw stiffened. 'You are testing my patience, little boy! Don't make this harder than it needs to be. You have multiple guns pointing at you. There's no escape. Don't play the hero.'

Charlie held his nerve, even though he felt his heart racing wildly in his chest. 'Go ahead – shoot me. See if I care. If you do, I can promise you'll never see your crystal again!'

Salvador snarled. 'Alright, Charles, we'll do it your way – bring me the girl!' he ordered.

Lurking in the shadows, one of Salvador's henchmen, dressed in a black suit and an earpiece, stood beside one of the vehicles. He threw open the rear door and pulled someone out. He dragged them into the bright light and tore a bag off their head.

Bridget, who looked terrified, stood with her hands tied together. She glanced around in bewilderment and finally locked eyes with Charlie. She attempted to run towards him, but the henchman yanked her back by her arm.

Bridget yelped. 'CHARLIE, HELP ME, PLEASE!' she cried.

'Let her go, you scumbag!' Charlie yelled, inching forward, feeling anger rise inside him as the henchman stood there grinning.

'See, Charles, I told you your friend was in good hands.' Salvador laughed mockingly. 'Now, you have wasted enough of my time already. Either tell me what you've done with my crystal or you and your pretty little friend here won't live to see the morning sun!'

Charlie snatched his walkie-talkie from his belt and held it in the air. 'You do that, and the cops will be here faster than your stupid space rocket can take off!' he threatened. 'My friend's waiting on standby, ready to go to the cops and tell them everything about your plan – unless he hears from me within the next two minutes!'

A look of anger crossed Salvador's face. 'I may have underestimated you, Charles. Lower your weapons.'

The red dots vanished from Charlie's chest.

Charlie breathed a sigh of relief, but he knew the trouble was far from over.

'I think we've got off on the wrong foot here,' Salvador said, changing his tune. 'I tell you what, how 'bout I release your friend just as soon as you tell me where—'

Salvador was interrupted by the sound of heavy footsteps heading towards them: the kind of footsteps that sounded mechanical, not like an ordinary person. Then from the darkness there emerged a soldier wearing an exosuit, holding something in one hand and someone by the scruff of their neck with the other.

It only took Charlie a second to realise who was being dragged along by the soldier. His face blanched with horror.

Salvador grinned wickedly. 'Well, what do we have here?'

The soldier brought the boy before Salvador. He looked pretty shaken up, his glasses were missing, and he was mumbling inaudibly. The soldier's helmet retracted to reveal his face; it was the soldier the children had seen in the forest.

'Whizzy...' Charlie whispered.

'I caught him wandering around outside the building with *this*,' said the soldier in a raspy voice, and threw Whizzy's walkie-talkie to Salvador.

Salvador sniggered. 'Hello, can you hear me, Charles?' he said. 'Oh dear, it doesn't seem to be working. Typical Chinese crap!' He dropped it and stamped on it several times, leaving it in pieces.

Salvador spun around to speak to Whizzy.

'So you're the boy who hacked into my company? Impressive, I must say, for a child, though I do have one question for you, Cody – or should I call you Whizzy? I'm curious to know, how long did it take you to hack into Amspatrax?' He bent down to place his ear close to Whizzy's mouth.

Whizzy continued mumbling to himself. By the look on Salvador's face, he didn't have a clue what Whizzy was muttering. Salvador grabbed Whizzy by the face and dug his nails into his cheeks. Charlie looked on, helpless and aghast.

'I asked you a question, you bumbling little parasite,' Salvador said, his eyes flashing with evil.

'Leave him alone!' Charlie yelled.

Salvador slowly turned his head, his eyes darkening. 'What did you say?' he said.

Charlie swallowed. 'I'll tell you where the crystal is – just leave my friend alone.'

Salvador released Whizzy, leaving Whizzy holding his jaw, and stood up straight. Casually he strolled over to Charlie and stood before him. 'Last chance, Charles. Where's my crystal?' he said.

Charlie sighed deeply. His plan to save Bridget had failed and now he had placed both his friends in jeopardy. He felt he had no choice but to tell Salvador where the crystal was, if they stood a chance of walking away. 'It's in Whizzy's backpack,' he said reluctantly.

'Ramus,' said Salvador, 'check the boy!'

Ramus, who stood behind Whizzy, snatched the backpack from his back, unzipped it, tipped it upside down and shook everything out. A tin box pinged against the ground. Ramus picked it up and inspected it. 'It's locked!' he exclaimed, turning to Salvador.

Salvador's face smouldered with anger. 'Where's the key, Charles?' he growled.

For the life of him, Charlie couldn't remember where he had put the key, and frantically began to check his pockets. He turned to Salvador with a look of dread. 'I-I-I don't have it.'

'Ramus!' barked Salvador.

Ramus cocked his gun and pointed it to the back of Whizzy's head. Whizzy stood there, cowering.

Charlie drew a sharp breath. He found himself screaming, 'NO!' but what he actually heard was Bridget yelling at the top of her lungs, 'I HAVE IT, I HAVE IT!'

'WAIT!' Salvador yelled at the soldier, who lowered his gun. Salvador looked at Bridget. 'Do you have something you wish to say to me, little girl?'

'I have it, I have the key!' said Bridget, fumbling around in her pocket.

Charlie glanced at Whizzy and found him squinting upwards; he had gone back to mumbling. Whizzy's behaviour made Charlie wonder what was wrong with him. Whizzy looked terrified, as if something terrible was worrying him – worse than the dire predicament they were in. Charlie was attempting to catch Whizzy's attention when a blue light filled the building.

Salvador had unlocked the box using the key Bridget had given him.

Everyone shaded their eyes – all except Salvador, who gazed deep into the crystal with a look of evil intent. His eyes sparkled like blue wildfire. He watched the energy swirl like the cosmos inside the crystal, and grinned devilishly.

'Remarkable, isn't it? All that power in such a small object,' he said, admiring the crystal. 'I will bring this world to its knees. Ramus!'

'Yes, boss,' answered the soldier behind Whizzy.

'Bring me my suit. We have a war to start!' said Salvador.

'You two,' Ramus said, turning to other soldiers in exosuits who were standing beside the vehicles, 'you heard the boss. Fetch him his suit – now!'

Moments later a floating transportation pod appeared, hovering above the ground. It was very long and had a shiny white outer casing and a translucent front panel, which emitted a gentle yellow glow.

Charlie's eyes grew wide. He was distracted by the levitating pod and didn't notice the little man behind it, wearing a lab technician's coat. The little man hurried along, trying to keep up. Charlie only noticed him when he saw a ball of fuzzy greyish hair bounce along on the other side of the pod. Once the pod stopped, the little man waddled around it, holding an electronic pad.

In the presence of Salvador, the little man looked nervous, wringing his hands. Before he spoke, he cleared his throat. 'Salvador, sir, might I suggest we run some preliminary tests first with the Blue Star and Robonik before you engage?'

'There's no time for that,' Salvador growled at him. 'The Russians have threatened me with dire consequences if I don't deliver the next generation of battle suits to them by tomorrow. The war must begin at once!'

'B-b-but, sir, I beg of you. Trying to harness the crystal's energy and use it to power the Robonik suit when we still don't know the full extent of its powers is madness! It may lead to catastrophic consequences. If you could just give me a little more time...' the little man pleaded.

Salvador cut him off by pulling a handgun from his waistband and aiming it at the man's head. The little man quaked in his shoes.

'One more word from you, Errold, and I will shorten your life expectancy of forty-two to thirty-two in an instant! Now go and prepare my suit for engagement!'

'What d'you want us to do with the children, boss?' Ramus enquired.

Salvador removed his suit jacket and began to loosen his tie. 'Shame your bumbling friend's skills weren't put to better use, Charles. He could've excelled somewhere like Amspatrax. Too bad you know so much about things you shouldn't. We need to dispose of you now.'

The children screamed and yelled, pleading for their lives to be spared, but Salvador showed no mercy. He simply gave them a wicked smile as they were dragged away. However, the soldiers stopped in their tracks, and not because of the children's pleas. A loud bang echoed around the building. It came from high above, as if something had landed on the roof. Then it happened again.

All the soldiers and henchmen pointed their weapons upwards into the darkness, while the three friends huddled together. A clang sounded again, leaving everyone on edge.

'I'm scared,' Bridget said, cowering beside Charlie.

'What's going on?' said Charlie, his eyes searching the darkness for answers.

'I-it's them,' Whizzy stuttered, still looking overcome by shock.

'Who's them?' Charlie asked in a whisper. 'Tell us who's up there. Is it the police?'

'No! It's A, A, A, ALIENS!' Whizzy spluttered. Those who heard him turned to cast sceptical looks upon him, while Charlie and Bridget stood thunderstruck by the revelation.

'What did you just say?' asked Salvador incredulously.

Whizzy could not say anything further. There was another bang, and the three of them jumped. Something was moving around up there. They all listened closely as the roof creaked and rattled.

'Ramus,' Salvador said, 'take a team and check it out. I have a sneaking suspicion we may have some unexpected guests.'

'You two – with me!' Ramus ordered two other soldiers. They were about to head off when, without warning, there was a deafening explosion and the roof came crashing down on them.

CHAPTER 10

BIG TROUBLE IN LITTLE VALLEY

L ying among the rubble, covered in dirt, Charlie finally came around, dazed and coughing. At first, he wasn't sure how long he'd been lying there or what had happened. But he realised what had occurred the moment he staggered to his feet and peered around.

The building looked as if a bomb had struck it. There were heaps of twisted and mangled steel and debris aflame everywhere. Charlie felt fortunate to be alive, though the same couldn't be said for the person beside him. He was lying face-down on the ground, dead. When Charlie saw him, he leapt backwards.

It was Salvador's henchman, the one who had been holding Bridget.

Charlie looked away from the unpleasant sight. He had started to search for Bridget when he heard footsteps close by. Someone was moving cautiously among the piles of debris.

At first, he could only see a shadowy figure through the murky light, until eventually they came closer and he could see them. At first, he thought it was one of Salvador's soldiers in an exosuit. However, this presumption was dashed when the soldier turned to face Charlie. Through their smoked-glass helmet, he saw their haunting and ghastly head.

There was no way it could've been one of Salvador's soldiers. What human could possibly look as pale as the moon, have holes instead of ears and nose on their hairless face, have a weave of bumps protruding over their head, and a broad jaw packed tightly with little sharp teeth, like a piranha's? Not to mention the bulging black wasp-like eyes that were staring right at him. There was no mistaking what it was; Charlie knew he was staring at an alien.

The creature wore grey battle armour and stood on two hind legs, like those of a faun. It held some kind of weapon, lit with blue lights. The alien took aim at him. Charlie tried to run, but his legs wouldn't move.

Charlie was doomed.

At that precise moment a small voice let out a desperate cry for help. Charlie and the alien creature turned to look at what had made the noise.

It was Bridget.

She was trapped beneath a pile of broken timber. The alien swung its weapon away from Charlie and aimed at Bridget instead.

'No!' cried Charlie.

As luck would have it, two soldiers in exosuits appeared from nowhere and shot at the alien creature. While this was going on, Charlie felt the life return to his numb legs, and he ran over to Bridget. He pulled the timber off her and pulled her free. He then led her away as quickly as possible. Shots were flying in all directions. He took her to a nearby wall, and they crouched down behind it.

'Are you okay, Bridget?' Charlie said.

'What the hell was that thing?' Bridget said, looking shocked.

'I have no idea,' replied Charlie, peering nervously around the wall. 'And it's probably best that we don't hang around to find out!'

'Wait, Charlie – I can't move my hands. They're still tied,' cried Bridget.

Charlie glanced down. 'Don't worry, I'll have you free in a sec.' From his backpack he pulled out his father's pocketknife. 'Hold still. I don't want to cut you.'

Bridget's hands were trembling.

Charlie sliced through the tape in one go and Bridget immediately flung her arms around him. He hugged her tightly and felt overwhelming joy fill his heart. He was reunited with his best friend.

'I'm so sorry about everything that's happened to you, Bridget,' he said. 'I should have listened to you. If we make it out of here, I understand if you don't want to be my friend any more.'

'You'll always be my friend, pea-brain,' Bridget said, pulling away and smiling, 'even if you do stupid things from time to time.'

'Speaking of friends, we need to find Whizzy and—'

There was a whoosh from above, then another explosion. The children jumped. An enormous hole had been blown in the roof. It was bigger than a circus tent. Through it, they saw to their horror hundreds of dazzling, flashing lights ... coming from an alien spacecraft.

'You got to be kidding me!' muttered Charlie.

'Oh my,' said Bridget.

Out of nowhere a swarm of aliens clattered around the edges of the hole and started shooting at everyone below with laser guns. Salvador's men returned fire. All hell broke loose and a war started between the aliens and the soldiers. Bridget shrieked as sparks flew and explosions shook the building. To make matters worse, the aliens started leaping through the hole and landing below: their legs seemed to act like springs, able to land on the floor far below effortlessly.

Caught in the crossfire, the two children scurried off in search of Whizzy, keeping low to the ground. Luckily, they soon found him, lying beneath a sheet of corrugated steel. Charlie lifted the sheet up, praying he was alive. He pushed it away and knelt down to place his ear against Whizzy's face.

Bridget gasped. 'Is he alive?'

'He's alive!' said Charlie, and he shook him vigorously by the shoulder. 'Wake up, Whizzy, wake up!'

It took a second for Whizzy to come around. When he did, his eyes were rolling around in the back of his head. 'Mom, is that you? The bad men are trying to kill me,' he mumbled.

'I'm not your mom!' Charlie said. 'It's me, Charlie!'

'Is it really you, Charlie? Thank goodness, for a second there I thought you were Salvador trying to kill me,' said Whizzy.

'We've got bigger problems than him,' exclaimed Charlie. 'You were right all along, Whizzy. Aliens really do exist, and they've arrived here in Little Valley!'

Whizzy sprang to his feet. 'I don't suppose they're friendly, are they?'

Charlie and Bridget shook their heads vehemently.

''Bout as friendly as a swarm of mosquitos. They must be here for the crystal. We need to get out of here!' said Charlie. He glanced around, searching for a way out, and spotted an unlit doorway some feet away. 'This way, you guys!' he yelled, pointing to it.

The children made their escape and fled down a dark corridor. They turned one corner, then another, only to find their path blocked by rubble. They turned and headed in the other direction, where they encountered an alien creature, its back to them. Bridget screamed, alerting the alien to their presence, and it fired off a laser shot. *BZZT!* It narrowly missed the children and blew a hole in the wall behind them.

The children ran for their lives, back up the corridor and out into the chaos of the battle. Unknown to them, there was an alien lurking on a steel platform above. It saw the children and fired off a shot, which skimmed past Charlie's head and struck a concrete pillar behind him. The bottom of the pillar crumbled, and it began to topple. At that precise moment, the alien that had chased the children up the corridor came tearing out of the doorway and ran into the path of the falling pillar. The pillar crushed the alien.

The three children dived behind a heap of steel to shelter from the shooting alien. Every time a laser blast struck nearby, Bridget yelped. In the end she covered her ears and closed her eyes to block out the noise.

'What we gonna do, Charlie?' Whizzy shouted, his voice trembling with fear. 'Those things are everywhere – we're trapped!'

Charlie looked at his two best friends in despair. What were they to do? They were surrounded by shooting aliens and piles of rubble. There was no way out. He peered cautiously through the gaps in the steel up at the platform. The alien creature was still lurking up there, keeping a watchful eye on them.

Gunfire and explosions continued to ring out.

As Charlie was about to turn away, out of the corner of his eye he saw something blue, glittering faintly, lying on the ground not far from them.

'No! Could it be?' Charlie said, his eyes widening. A glimmer of hope filled him, along with one of his crazy ideas. *If that's what I think it is, then maybe...*

'Hey, guys, come here.' He waved them over. 'Look!'

Bridget peeked through the tiny gap in the steel.

'It's the crystal!' she gasped.

'I'll take your word for it,' said Whizzy.

'If I can get to it, then perhaps I can use Salvador's suit to get us out of here! What do you reckon?' Charlie suggested.

Bridget narrowed her eyes. 'Seriously? Have you lost your mind?' she said. 'That thing's the reason we're in this mess to begin with!'

'I'm with Bridget on this one,' Whizzy said. 'Are you forgetting what happened the last time you touched it?'

'I know, and you're right, but you heard what Salvador said – it can be controlled using the suit he made,' Charlie argued.

'How can you be so sure?' said Bridget. 'Like that little man said, they hadn't even tested it yet. What if you die? Then what?'

'Do you have any better ideas? Because I'm all out,' Charlie snapped. 'Sorry. Look, I know you're scared, and I am too, but we're sitting ducks. Sooner or later Salvador's men or the aliens are gonna find us, and when they do we're toast! We can't hide here forever.'

Bridget and Whizzy exchanged a look.

'Alright, alright,' Bridget grumbled. 'If it means us getting out of this nightmare, and then I can go back to living a boring life watching *Bonnie*, then I'm in!'

Charlie was taken back by Bridget's response; even Whizzy looked surprised. It was rare for the two of them to agree on things. Charlie met her approval with a half-hearted smile. He turned to Whizzy. 'You know, our pack vote only requires two of us to agree to make a decision, right?'

'I know,' replied Whizzy, looking disappointed. 'Two to one, I get it.'

'Not any more,' Charlie said, shaking his head. 'From now on, no decision will be taken unless the three of us agree on it, okay? So the final vote rests with you, Whizzy. We either do this or we don't. If we don't, we'll just have to find some other way.'

Whizzy hesitated. 'I don't see how I can be much help here. I can't see squat without my glasses.'

'Glasses or not, you're a part of this team,' Bridget said, placing her hand on Whizzy's shoulder to reassure him. 'Right, Charlie?'

'Too right you are!' Charlie said earnestly. 'We're a team and we stick together. We need you, Whizzy, so what do you say? Are you in?' Charlie held his hand out. Bridget placed hers on top of his.

The look on Whizzy's face suggested he still wasn't convinced. 'You know, all my life I've wanted to meet an extra-terrestrial, and now they've finally arrived here on Earth, I've changed my mind.' He placed his hand on top of theirs. 'I'm in.'

Charlie smiled. 'Alright! Listen up – here's what we need to do.'

CHAPTER 11

PLAN B

'You know this is a bad idea, right?' Whizzy stammered to Bridget.

Bridget was beside Whizzy, clutching a broken rod she'd found. The pair were crouched behind a heap of mangled steel waiting for Charlie, who was spying between the cracks, to give them the signal.

Charlie's Plan B was for Bridget and Whizzy to distract the alien loitering on the platform for long enough so that Charlie could recover the crystal. Then he would set off in search of the pod containing the suit. Once he had found them both, he would return to help the three of them escape.

It was a risky strategy. Nevertheless, a risk worth taking, in his eyes. What other choice did they have? Soon or later they were either going to be captured or killed. And if Salvador found the crystal, then his plan to start a war would inevitably continue. Something had to be done. Someone had to put a stop to it. That 'someone',

Charlie felt, was him. However, there was one other problem to contend with – apart from not knowing where the suit was in the labyrinth of steel and debris. The alien invaders themselves.

'You don't need to remind me,' Bridget hissed at him, 'but, like Charlie said, if we don't do something, we're as good as dead anyway!'

'I find the dead part inconceivable,' said Whizzy, sinking to the floor, 'but we can't just sit here waiting for him to come back. What if something happens to him and he doesn't return? What then?'

Bridget stared into the shadows, looking worried. She was looking towards the dead alien that had been crushed by the fallen pillar. It was still holding its weapon. When Bridget saw this her eyes went wide with curiosity.

'I have an idea!' she said excitedly, turning to Whizzy.

Whizzy didn't have a chance to ask her what it was, for Charlie turned around and said, 'Okay, you guys, you ready?'

They looked as if they were about to pass out from fright, but they nodded.

'It'll be fine. I promise I'll come straight back as soon as I've got the crystal and the suit. Just make sure you keep well hidden. Okay, ready, three, two, one, go!' Charlie yelled.

Whizzy leapt out from behind the pile of rubble and started to yell and wave his hands in the air. However, he was the only one who did. Bridget was supposed to join him, but she had other intentions. She crawled across the ground on her hands and knees in the direction of the dead alien, to retrieve its gun. The alien on the platform stopped firing in the other direction and started to shoot at Whizzy.

BZZT, BZZT, WHOOTASH, WHOOTASH!

The lasers missed Whizzy by a whisker. Luckily, Bridget got back in the nick of time to pull him to safety. They covered their heads as the laser blasts ricocheted all around, showering them in a rain of hot metal.

'Where did you go? You were supposed to – jeez!' Whizzy said, gawping at the weapon Bridget was holding. 'Where did you get that?'

'How does this thing work?' she said, looking frustrated as she fiddled with the gun.

'What are you going to do with that?' Whizzy asked, looking concerned.

Bridget pressed a button on the side of the gun and it powered up. She turned to Whizzy. 'Keep us alive.'

In the meantime, Charlie was scurrying in and out the shadows between the towering piles of ruins. He snuck around the side of the platform, where he found the crystal lying in the dirt. He scooped it up and put it in his pocket, along with a pile of earth.

With it now back in his possession, he headed to search for the pod, turning this way and that, doing his utmost to avoid the aliens. But the closer he got to the centre of the battle, the greater the danger became. And it wasn't long before he ran into serious trouble.

An alien descended from the opening in the roof right in front of him. The alien fired, and the shot missed Charlie's foot by inches. His heart in his mouth, Charlie turned and bolted in the other direction, only to be faced by another alien. With the aliens closing in on him, Charlie searched frantically for an escape route ... then he saw a dark hole in a mound of rubble.

Charlie didn't hesitate. He flung himself into the small hole, which turned out to be a buried ventilation shaft. He slithered along in the dark like a snake for a short time, then he reached the other end and fell out onto the ground. He could hear and see bullets and laser blasts streaming through the air in every direction. Between the piles of entangled twisted metal and bricks, he saw sparks of gunfire: it was Salvador's men.

Charlie gazed up at the lights coming from the roof. An army of aliens was descending like raindrops from the sky. 'We're all doomed if I don't hurry up and find that suit!' he said to himself.

A few feet away, a single headlight shone. It cast a dim glow over something lying on the ground, shining a pearly white. Charlie ran over. He brushed the dirt away from the glass to reveal the pod, half buried beneath a mound of rubble. The pod was no longer in pristine condition, and its lights flickered.

Charlie's eyes lit up in jubilation. The suit was still there!

Quickly, he began to remove the stones one by one. He was trying to prise the pod open with his hands when a small voice yelled at him, 'WHAT D'YOU THINK YOU'RE DOING? GET AWAY FROM THERE!'

Charlie froze.

He turned around and saw, to his surprise, Errold, Salvador's scientist, a few yards away, staggering to his feet. Bizarrely, Charlie hadn't noticed him lying there until now. By the look of it, he had been hit over the head by something, because down the front of his balding head was a finger-long gash and a streak of blood.

Seemingly oblivious to the chaos that was all around them, Errold stood there swaying giddily, concentrating on correcting his bent glasses, which had been twisted. He was muttering angrily to himself about his not-so-white lab coat as he dusted himself off. Errold seemed to have forgotten about Charlie, because he began searching around his feet, as if he was looking for something important.

Charlie watched anxiously as Errold waddled over to pick an electronic control pad off the ground. Errold jolted and leapt into the air as a laser blast struck the ground beside him.

'Great Scott!' Errold said, turning to stare at the glittering light above.

Charlie stared at the control lying on the ground and wondered whether he could use it to unlock the pod. So, while the little man was distracted, Charlie discreetly edged closer. However, Errold turned to look at him.

'You have no business being here,' Errold warned. 'If I were you, I would leave while you still have the chance.'

'And stand by and let that megalomaniac start a war? It's not gonna happen!'

Errold watched Charlie glance at the control pad on the ground. His tiny eyes flashed behind his glasses.

They both darted for the device. Charlie got there first, then Errold jumped on his back. Charlie tried to shake him off, but Errold wouldn't let go.

'Give it here!' Errold yelled, pulling Charlie's backpack from him and wrapping his baby-like arms around his neck.

Charlie frantically pressed as many buttons as he could on the electronic device, but nothing seemed to work.

Was the device broken? he thought.

Then suddenly, a high-pitched *pssssttttt* made the pair look up in surprise. The glass panel on the pod was wide open. It had worked! Charlie beamed with delight; Errold's face, however, was filled with dread.

'Oh, Salvador's going to be mad when he learns you've opened up the pod to his precious Robonik suit!' said Errold.

Charlie flung the little man off him, but Errold sprang at him and grabbed Charlie by his legs.

'Let – go – of – me!' Charlie cried and kicked out, booting Errold in the head. Errold let out a yelp of pain and fell back, holding his face.

Charlie dragged himself along the floor to the pod and peered in. There it was, the magnificent Robonik suit, its diamond-shaped mesh shimmering. A helmet was next to it. Charlie stared at it in awe. Admittedly, it did look rather big for him. Nevertheless, it was every bit as impressive as the one he had seen on Whizzy's computer. Charlie slowly extended his arm to touch it, when a screeching alien appeared behind him and fired off a laser shot.

The powerful blast skimmed past Charlie's head, struck the pod, and sent them both spinning in the air. The pod hit the ground with a thud, as did Charlie, rendering him semi-conscious.

Charlie lay on his back, feeling pain shooting up and down his body. He feared that at any second now the alien would come and finish him off. The alien strode awkwardly towards him, but it didn't look the least bit interested in him; it headed towards something else instead. Charlie rolled his head to the side to see, to his utter horror, the Blue Star. It had fallen out of his pocket and was lying on the ground.

All hope was lost.

The alien leaned down to grab the crystal with its three tentacle-like fingers. There was a huge *BOOM*. The alien's body went limp and it fell to the ground.

Charlie felt his lungs finally expand to their maximum capacity after what felt like an eternity of not being able to breathe, and for a split second he wondered who – or what – had killed the alien. But he needed to get to the crystal. He crawled painfully along the ground, dragging his injured leg behind him, and reached out to the Blue Star.

'ARRGGHH!' Charlie squealed suddenly.

His fingertips were within inches of grabbing the crystal when a big black shoe covered in dust stamped on his hand, pinning it to the floor. There was no mistaking whose shoe it was.

It was Salvador's.

'Trying to steal from me again, are we, Charles?' Salvador said. Errold was back on his feet and stood, cowering, beside Salvador, looking sorry for himself and holding his bloodied face.

Salvador peered sharply at him. 'Something the matter, Errold?'

'That boy – he broke my nose!' cried Errold.

'An improvement, I dare say.' Salvador snickered.

'Yes, well, if I hadn't stopped him, he would have stolen your Robonik suit!'

'Is that so?' Salvador glared down at Charlie with hatred in his eyes, continuing to apply pressure to Charlie's hand. He squealed in agony.

'You really are becoming a pain in the backside, Charles. I think it's high time you were taught a lesson: it's wrong to take things that don't belong to you!'

He pointed the barrel of his shotgun at Charlie and curled his finger around the trigger. Just then several aliens advanced around the side of a burning mound of debris, shooting. One of the shots managed to strike Salvador in the arm. He fell to the ground, crying out in agony. Salvador's head soldier, Ramus, came up over the top of the buried vehicles and returned fire. Salvador slid away, leaving a trail of blood behind him. Errold did not hang around. He turned to make a run for it, but was pursued by one of the aliens, who went chasing after him.

While all this was going on, Charlie rolled sideways, managing to land on top of the Blue Star. Without thinking, he picked it up and crawled to safety under the pod, which had been flipped upside down and was now resting on its hinges like an open coffin. Charlie crawled underneath.

The only light was the faint light that came from the Blue Star. Charlie trembled inside the dark pod as he listened to the dull sound of gunfire, then he saw, to his surprise, the Robonik suit. It was still there, though lying on the ground as if it had been discarded like an old piece of clothing. The helmet was still fixed to the inside panel.

Charlie tried to put down the crystal so he could slip the helmet on, but for some reason he couldn't. Knowing what would happen if he continued to hold on to it, he started to panic. He tried to shake it loose and even attempted to prise his fingers open with his other hand, but nothing worked. His hand was firmly wrapped around the Blue Star, and there was no way of letting go.

It had become a life-or-death situation for him – and a race against time.

One way or another, he needed to get the suit on. With only one hand spare, this would be a challenge. Then he realised there appeared to be no zip or buttons to undo on the suit. How could he put it on?

'You got to be kidding me!' he said in disbelief.

Charlie quickly slid the helmet on, then wrestled with the Robonik suit, putting one foot through the neck, while the Blue Star glowed dangerously in his hand.

Fear was driving Charlie on: the fear of Salvador or the aliens coming to kill him. The fear of failing, failing his friends, who trusted him and believed in him. But worst of all, if he failed, his family could be placed in terrible danger from the alien invasion, should they have come to conquer Earth. The more emotional Charlie grew, the brighter the crystal glowed.

From under the pod blue lights came sprawling like tendrils, touching and reaching out to everything in sight, as far away as Bridget and Whizzy. Bridget stopped firing at aliens, who she'd been picking off discreetly, and she and Whizzy stared in wonder at a dome of blue electrical energy that was growing bigger by the second.

'Er, is it me or has everything in here gone blue suddenly?' Whizzy remarked.

Bridget gasped. 'Charlie!'

The aliens ceased firing at the men. They moved towards the blue light and directed all their firepower at its source, but their lasers did not penetrate the light. Then something truly incredible happened. In a blink of an eye, the electrical storm shrank to nothing, then an explosion of energy cast out a ring of white light, rocking the building and bowling everyone to the ground. Bridget and Whizzy shakily climbed to their feet and stood in the eerie silence that filled the building. They feared the worst.

Was Charlie still alive?

CHAPTER 12

CHARLIE ROBONIK

The enormous swelling of the electromagnetic energy field made the transportation pod that Charlie was hiding beneath disintegrate. Now he lay there exposed, curled up in a foetal position for all to see. Strangely, though, he wasn't wearing the clothes he had set out in that night – his jeans and hoodie. Instead, he was wearing the Robonik exosuit.

All up and down the black mesh suit, blue sparks surged. By some miracle, Charlie had managed to absorb the dangerous energy from the blue crystal by donning the suit and, in doing so, had stopped himself from exploding. It was a good job he had succeeded. Had he failed, he would have blown up like and killed everything around him. Nonetheless, the averted disaster brought about a ceasefire. The aliens started to gather around, their expressions docile.

When Charlie's eyes opened for the first time since he had transitioned into something more than a human, he saw in his peripheral vison a virtual interface. On it were the words OPTIMISING WITH HOST, with a progress bar at 59 per cent. Charlie assumed he was seeing this information from inside Salvador's helmet. He only realised he wasn't wearing the helmet when he absentmindedly touched his throbbing head. The helmet had disintegrated when his body had transitioned it.

Charlie was mystified. He didn't have the faintest notion what had happened to him. Behaving like a new-born calf, he tried to stand up. He didn't make it much further than his hands and knees before falling back down to the ground. He breathed heavily, exhausted, and continued to stare, bewildered, at the progress bar, which it had moved to 63 per cent. He wondered what would happen when it reached 100 per cent. He attempted to wipe it away, but it didn't work. When he did this, he discovered that his hand was ... shimmering. In fact, he was shimmering all over. He wore a black mesh suit with neon-blue rivulets flowing between the diamond shapes.

'I'm wearing the Robonik suit!' he said, flabbergasted. 'But how?'

Rubbing his fingers together, he examined the texture of the suit. It felt incredible, as if he was touching his own skin. Behind his hand he saw something move, and looked at it. Charlie felt his stomach sink. A throng of aliens were moving in silence towards him. Then, to his surprise, they stopped and came no further.

Fearing what they were going to do to him, Charlie tried to rise from the ground once more. He finally managed, and stood, his knees wobbling – out of weakness rather than fright. He looked around at the vast number of aliens surrounding him; there were more than he could count.

Charlie gulped.

All the aliens stood stock-still, glaring at him, their weapons by their sides. But why weren't they attacking him? Charlie was nonplussed.

The place had turned eerily quiet. There was no sound of bullets or lasers whizzing through the air, no sound of destruction or falling debris – nothing. In fact, the quietness felt stranger to Charlie than the battle he had been caught up in. A long silence followed. But from it an unusual sound grew. It didn't come abruptly but grew subtly, as if it were already there. It didn't change in loudness. Charlie had never heard such a peculiar sound before in his life. It was so unfamiliar, he had nothing to compare it to. It sounded like a soft, high-pitched chiming on a continuous note. It felt as if something was about to materialise.

As if by magic, a glittering light grew from within the air. It swirled and sparkled in an array of colours, changing in size before Charlie's eyes. The larger it grew, the darker it became. As Charlie stood there, mesmerised, a figure walked out of the light as if it were stepping through a doorframe. The glittering light vanished as quickly as it had come, but the monstrous alien that emerged didn't. Charlie gasped incredulously. It was terrifying.

It wore a different kind of body armour to the others, in a greenish black, and was much bigger than the rest of them. It was so heavy, Charlie could feel the ground tremble beneath his feet as it walked towards him. All the aliens cried out in an unearthly harmony, as if to acknowledge their leader.

If this is their General, I'm done for, Charlie thought.

Charlie thought of running away as fast as he could from the nightmare. But it was impossible, for his legs were like jelly. Plus, there was nowhere to run, even if he could. The aliens had him surrounded. Charlie looked around to see if there was anyone who could possibly help him, but none of the soldiers were anywhere to be seen. Nor was Salvador, for that matter. Though he did pray that his best friends were still alive.

Charlie was so shaken by the hulking figure standing before him that he couldn't bring himself to look up at first. But finally he did. The faceless alien General stared down at him. Charlie's heart stuttered. The alien

General, who wore a helmet, seemed to be examining Charlie, but what it did next took Charlie by surprise.

The monstrous overlord grabbed Charlie by the throat and lifted him high above its head, with very little effort. Charlie squirmed and flapped around like a fish out of water, gasping for breath. The alien creature made an unearthly sound, as if it were angrily saying something to him, then lurched forward and let go of Charlie. He fell to the ground, holding his painful neck. The alien General had turned away. Charlie caught a glimpse of a small hole that had been singed through the armour plating on its right shoulder.

How did that happen? Charlie wondered.

Glancing past the General, Charlie saw in the distance a small figure running along a high metal walkway.

'Bridget?' he breathed, staring in disbelief.

The General cried out. The aliens reacted like a colony of aggravated fire ants and went on the attack, hunting Bridget down.

A surge of panic tore through Charlie. He needed to help his friends, but he was so weak that he didn't have the strength to crawl away to save himself. The crystal had sucked every ounce of energy from him and had left him feeling as though he was dying. He blinked, which brought up the progress bar. It stood at 95 per cent.

Charlie vaguely remembered Salvador saying something about how a neurocranial transmitter built into the helmet could connect with A.L.I.C.E., but how was that possible when he was no longer wearing the helmet? He gave up the struggle, and let his head rest on the ground. He listened with dread as the ground started to vibrate. The alien General was beside him.

The progress bar moved again: 96 per cent. Charlie watched anxiously. Whatever was likely to happen once it reached 100 per cent, he prayed it would save him from his terrible fate. Charlie gazed at the General's metal boot before looking up at it. In its six-fingered hand, the alien General held a dark grey stout metal rod inscribed with what looked like weird hieroglyphics. The alien pressed a button and spikes shot out from either end of the rod. It had turned into a telescopic spear. The pointy silver tip caught the light from the alien spaceship and sparkled cruelly.

The progress bar did not falter: 97 per cent, 98 per cent, 99 per cent.

The alien General raised the spear into the air. Charlie took a final look at the message, which read:

OPTIMISATION COMPLETE WITH HOST.

'Hello, Charles,' a womanly robotic voice said to him.

Suddenly, Charlie felt an atomic explosion of energy within him and the Robonik suit became electrically charged; it lit up a blinding blue like a power grid. Charlie's body shook uncontrollably. No longer did it feel like his brain was half-asleep – it had woken up.

The alien General hesitated. It watched as the Robonik suit mutated over Charlie's face to create a black mask. The General had seen enough. It thrust the spear into the air and brought it down with considerable force. At the last second, Charlie rolled out of harm's way and sprang to his feet, leaving the spear to embed itself in the ground. The alien General let out an infuriated roar.

Charlie stepped back with shock and uncertainty – not because of the alien, but because everything around him had drastically altered. No longer was he seeing through his own eyes. Now he could detect heat signatures and the motion of those in the building, and his eyes could zoom in like a camera. He could see his heart rate (which had elevated greatly) and his body temperature, as well as the air temperature around him, projected in the air in front of him.

'Hostile alien life form detected, Charles,' A.L.I.C.E. said, zooming in on the General, whose heat signature glowed orange.

'Who said that?' said Charlie, looking around.

'There is no time for questions, Charles. You must take action,' A.L.I.C.E. directed. With that, the alien General launched its spear and sent it soaring past Charlie's head, only missing him by inches.

'Warning: hostile alien engaged,' intoned A.L.I.C.E.

The hulking General charged like a raging bull towards Charlie and swung its mighty metal fist. Charlie ducked the blow and quickly came to realise he was amazingly fast. Unnaturally fast. But he was distracted by A.L.I.C.E. talking to him, and this allowed the alien General to land a blow so hard that it sent Charlie sailing through the air and through the brick wall of the building. He landed outside in a field, tumbling over and over again on the grass, then eventually came to rest flat on his back.

'Okay, that hurt!' He groaned.

'Analysing your vital signs. Task complete. You do not appear to have sustained any form of injury,' A.L.I.C.E. confirmed happily.

Charlie staggered to his feet and yelled, 'Who the hell are you? And why can I hear you inside my head?'

'I am A.L.I.C.E.,' said A.L.I.C.E. 'An Artificial Learning Intelligence Cybernetic Electronic system created by Dr Enoch Salvador in the year 1990 to serve as his personal assistant. You are able to hear me, Charles, for the energy you absorbed from the Blue Star corrupted my operating system and took control of me.'

'The helmet...' Charlie said, thinking aloud.

'That is correct. When you put it on, my operating power began to transfer to you and I was able to connect to your brain,' A.L.I.C.E. explained.

'So, what does this mean exactly?' Charlie said, confused.

'It means that I have become an entity within your mind. We are symbiotically connected, therefore I need you to survive. If you die, I will also be terminated,' said A.L.I.C.E.

'Wait a second. You mean I'm stuck with you inside my head for, like, forever?' Charlie said, horrified.

The *whump* of an explosion broke the night, and the field was torn up by the violent blast.

'Charles, I'm detecting aggression coming from the alien ship,' reported A.L.I.C.E.

'YOU DON'T SAY!' exclaimed Charlie, swerving a round of blasts as he ran towards a dilapidated hanger.

The ground exploded behind him and sent him catapulting through the air. He landed with a thud behind the hanger. Uninjured, he got to his feet. He peeped around the corner of the hanger, praying the spaceship had gone, when there was another giant blast, like a bolt of lightning. It took out half the side of the building – and almost him along with it. Charlie raced around to the other side of the building and stood panicking. It was only a matter of time. When the next thunderous blast came from the spaceship, he would be done for.

'Charles, I am picking up two human life forms inside the main building who are at risk of extermination,' A.L.I.C.E. said.

Charlie gasped. 'Bridget and Whizzy! I need to get back inside and help them!'

'In that case, I suggest you initiate Robonik battle mode, Charles,' advised A.L.I.C.E.

'Battle mode?' Charlie repeated, surprised. 'You're telling me this suit has a *battle mode*? Why didn't you say something before?'

'I am informing you now,' replied A.L.I.C.E. 'Using your symbiotic energy you have the ability to alter your physical structure. This is as a result of the nanobots that have entered your bloodstream.'

'How do I enter battle mode?' Charlie asked quickly.

'By thinking or vocalising the command,' said A.L.I.C.E.

'Well, hurry up and change me, for crying out loud!' ordered Charlie.

Nothing happened.

'I'm afraid the commands must be direct and simple,' A.L.I.C.E. informed him.

'Fine. Robonik, change to battle mode. Happy now?'

'Indubitably,' replied A.L.I.C.E.

Charlie watched in wonder as the black suit smoothly transformed into an armour-plated power suit.

'Whoa, check me out,' Charlie said, admiring himself. 'I'm twice the size I usually am!'

'Charles, I've located an entry point at the back of the building for you to regain access.'

A screen came up in front of Charlie's eyes, showing the terrain in front of him.

'That's no good. It's too far to run. I won't make it without being blown to smithereens by that flying saucer! There's gotta be a quicker way to get back in there.'

'There is another way that will place you directly where you were previously, but I do not recommend this, because you do not yet know how to power leap,' A.L.I.C.E. warned him.

'Power leap?' Charlie said, intrigued. 'You mean I can, like, jump high?'

'Indeed.'

A.L.I.C.E. displayed a red line starting from where Charlie was. It curved like a rainbow high up over the building.

'Be real, would you? How am I supposed to make that? I'm not fricking Superman, you know!'

'Use your mind to stimulate your symbiotic energy – feel it grow inside you. When you feel the energy start to build, release it in a short burst,' said A.L.I.C.E.

Charlie gazed at the roof and shook his head dismissively. 'I'll never make it. It's too far!'

'Two hundred and sixty-five feet, to be precise,' A.L.I.C.E. said helpfully.

Charlie snorted. 'Well, there's your answer. It's impossible!'

'Not impossible,' replied A.L.I.C.E. 'You are more than capable. You just aren't ready to make the leap without training first, Charles.'

'Stop calling me Charles, would you?' Charlie said, agitated. 'It's bad enough that I've gotta deal with you yapping inside my head – which, by the way, is still freaking me out. I don't need you sounding like my mom as well when she's annoyed at me!'

'What do you wish me to call you?' A.L.I.C.E. asked.

'Call me Charlie, okay?'

'As you command, Charlie.'

Another blast from the alien spaceship blew up the remainder of the hanger, leaving Charlie vulnerable. It was now or never. Charlie had to make the leap. He set his sights on the roof of the building and focused his mind. He crouched and felt a warm energy build inside him. A blue cloud of energy began to form, silhouetting him. As the energy grew stronger, the ground beneath his feet started to crack. Then, like releasing an elastic band, he let the energy explode. He shot into the air. At that moment a final blast came down from the alien spaceship and blew a hole in the ground right where Charlie had been standing.

'Woohoo, look at me! I'm flying!' he yelled, soaring high above the building.

As he started to descend through the hole in the roof, it soon became apparent to him that he was out of control and he plummeted pitched headfirst. He walloped into the ground. Dust billowed up around him. The alien General, who was standing yards away, turned to see Charlie lying on the ground.

'Gotta work on that landing for next time.' Charlie groaned.

'Perhaps you'll consider training first before attempting another long-distance jump,' said A.L.I.C.E.

'Thanks. I'll bear that in mind,' Charlie said, getting painfully to his feet.

The alien General drew a war axe from its back and took up a fighting stance. The axe had inscriptions all over it, just like the telescopic spear had.

'Charlie, your friends have retreated into a small room at the back of the building,' said A.L.I.C.E., displaying a 3D layout of the building and their location for Charlie. 'You must hurry. They will not survive long.'

Charlie stared at the hulking General, who stood between him and his friends, and charged towards it. The alien General didn't hesitate. It bellowed then went thundering towards him. Both hands gripped around the hilt of the enormous axe, the monstrous alien swung it with all its might. Charlie anticipated the General's actions and timed it perfectly, dropping to his knees at the last second and sliding underneath the swooping axe.

'You know, you should really work on that. I've seen a better swing on a porch!' Charlie heckled the General as he ran off.

Charlie fought countless aliens along the way to find his friends. While battling them, he discovered more and more about his new-found powers, such as his remarkable strength: he was able to pick up a huge broken piece of concrete and toss it in the air as if it was a beach ball. However, no matter how many aliens he fought, the swarm of invaders kept on coming.

'There's too many of them,' Charlie cried, crouching behind a concrete pillar. 'There's no way I can get through them all.'

'Charlie, you're running out of time. Your friends are about to be exterminated. You must get to them now,' warned A.L.I.C.E.

The chilling reminder sent a shiver down his spine. He glanced hopelessly at the screen. His hapless friends were barricaded in a small room. There was no escape for them; outside the door, the corridor was crawling with aliens.

Distracted by what he was seeing, Charlie didn't notice the alien sneaking up from behind until it grabbed him and slung him into a concrete wall. The wall cracked as he slammed into it. The alien reached for its weapon. Charlie grabbed it around the waist like a pro wrestler, picking it up and charging through the concrete wall. He ploughed through wall after wall with the alien before eventually stopping. By good luck, he was in the room where Bridget and Whizzy were holed up! He tossed the dead alien aside.

The sound of the wall exploding had startled the children. Bridget swung round and fired off a shot, which almost struck Charlie.

'Don't shoot, don't shoot!' Charlie cried, throwing his hands in the air.

Bridget's eyes widened with a look of disbelief. 'Charlie, is that you?'

'Yeah! It's me you guys!' Charlie said excitedly.

'Why does your voice sound so weird? Has it broken or something?' asked Whizzy, who couldn't see him.

At that moment, Charlie detected alien movement entering the room. 'GET DOWN!' he yelled.

The children hit the deck just as a blast from the alien's gun zapped over their heads and struck the back wall. Charlie kicked up onto his feet and tore towards the alien, which fired off another shot. However, for some bizarre reason the laser seemed to be travelling through the air at a snail's pace, as if time had slowed right down.

But it hadn't. Charlie had speeded up. His speedy reaction had drawn on his symbiotic energy, powering up his body to move so swiftly that he was a blur. Charlie tore past his friends and ran up the wall, pushed himself off it, cartwheeled over the laser and landed gracefully on the other side, facing the alien. His sudden burst of energy was spent; time reverted to normal. The laser hit the wall at the normal speed. Before the alien could react, Charlie kicked it back through the doorway.

When he turned around to face the other two, Bridget stood there, a dumbstruck look on her face and her mouth hanging open.

'You two okay?' Charlie asked, approaching them.

They nodded.

'C'mon, we need to—'

Suddenly, Charlie fell to the ground. He had been blasted in the back by another alien that had entered the room. Bridget returned fire and killed the alien. She tossed the gun aside and raced over to Charlie, who was lying face-down on the ground.

'Are you alright, Charlie?' Bridget asked, looking him up and down, not knowing what to do.

'Gah,' he replied, coming to his senses.

Charlie's suit was repairing itself as Bridget watched. 'There isn't a scratch on you,' she marvelled.

Charlie rose to his feet.

'Charlie, I've detected a large mass of aliens heading from the wall you've just run through. You must find a way out at once,' A.L.I.C.E said to him in his mind.

'Got it!' replied Charlie aloud.

'Who are you talking to?' Whizzy questioned.

'Guys, we need to get out of here. The aliens are heading this way and will be coming through that doorway any second now!' said Charlie urgently.

'But there's nowhere to go! The corridors are crawling with aliens!' Bridget pointed out.

Charlie glanced over Bridget's shoulder and scanned the wall, where the laser had created a hole as it passed through. A.L.I.C.E. confirmed it led to the outside.

'I have an idea,' he said. 'Stand back! I sure hope this works.'

The two stood aside and watched Charlie, mesmerised by his suit, which glowed a neon blue. A second later he went charging at the wall, his shoulder first, leaving a wavy blue flare of light trailing behind him. He ran straight through the wall, smashing a massive hole through to the outside.

'Quick, you guys, they're coming!' Charlie said, waving them through.

Charlie stood guard as his two friends clambered across the pile of broken bricks and dashed to the chain-link fence. They peeled back a broken section and slid through. Charlie had been worrying so much about the aliens bursting through the doorway at any moment, he'd completely forgotten about the spaceship.

When he attempted to bound over the fence, he heard a sonic boom. The blast struck the earth right where he stood.

A.L.I.C.E.'s warning came too late.

Charlie never saw it coming. The mammoth fireball blew him off his feet and sent him spinning in the air. He crashed to the ground and lay there, motionless.

CHAPTER 13

THE GUNSLINGER

Charlie was brought around by a high-pitched ringing. It was a terrible noise: it made him scrunch his eyes tightly together and clench his teeth, and it appeared to come from no particular direction. Rather, it seemed to encompass him. Being blasted by the alien spaceship had left Charlie wounded and confused. But amid his confusion he could hear a sharp voice yelling to him.

'Charlie, can you hear me? You need to get up. The alien ship is preparing to attack you again!'

'A.L.I.C.E.?' Charlie said dozily, realising whose voice it was. He shook his hazy head and looked up. The alien spaceship was slowly gliding in his direction. He rolled onto his back then leapt to his feet. Another blast came from the spaceship. Charlie saw it coming and took evasive action. He leapt sideways into a roll and sprang back up, prepared to dodge the next one, when he heard someone calling out to him. 'CHARLIE!'

Snapping his head around, Charlie saw his friends through the chain-link fence. 'You guys, what are you doing? You need to get out of here now!'

The two children didn't have time to heed Charlie's advice, for the alien spaceship opened fire in their direction. The blasts struck the earth only yards away and sent a flurry of mud raining down on their heads. Bridget and Whizzy screamed.

Before long the spaceship was directly above them. A large weapon materialised below the nose of the spaceship and took aim at the children. Bridget and Whizzy lay on the ground, frozen in fear, as the weapon armed itself, glowing a bright orange.

Charlie drew a sharp breath and looked at his friends, trapped near the fence. 'Help me, A.L.I.C.E., what do I do?' he beseeched her.

'Charlie, use your symbiotic energy to operate arm cannons,' advised A.L.I.C.E.

'Arm cannons?' he said, perplexed. 'How do I do that?'

'The same way you morphed into Robonik battle mode. Just think or say the words,' replied A.L.I.C.E. 'I must warn you, Charlie, that energy loss can have a negative effect on your health.'

'I couldn't care less what happens to me. All that matters is saving my friends!' cried Charlie.

Light along the side of the weapon lit up. Was it preparing to fire? When Charlie saw this, he didn't hesitate. 'Robonik, transform to arm cannons!' His forearms miraculously morphed into two cannons. Charlie stared, mesmerised, at them. 'Eat this!' he yelled and unloaded a plethora of blue energy balls at the spaceship.

SHAZACK, SHAZACK, BOOM, BOOM, SHAZACK, SHAZACK, BOOM, BOOM!

Blue flames exploded on the underside of the spaceship, immobilising the main weapon.

'Get out of here, you guys!' Charlie yelled to his friends.

Bridget and Whizzy scrambled to their feet and sprinted off into the night. It was fortunate they escaped when they did. The spaceship returned fire as it headed away. Its bullets struck an old drum beside the chain-link fence, which contained waste chemicals. The exploding drum started a chain reaction of exploding drums.

'Charlie, watch out!' A.L.I.C.E. called.

KABOOM! The yard went up in a giant ball of flames.

Diving out of harm's way, Charlie got back up sharpish, for the flames were licking against his armour. 'Help me, A.L.I.C.E.! I'm on fire!' he yelled.

'Charlie, your suit is impervious to fire. There is no need to worry,' said A.L.I.C.E.

'Oh,' he said, surprised.

Charlie hadn't noticed the aliens marching out of the hole in the side of building, until multiple flashes of orange lasers blistered past his head. Charlie kept his nerve, stood firm and fought back, and before long he was winning the battle.

Advanced as the aliens' weapons were, they were no match for Charlie's dual cannons. Countless aliens became the victims of his blue energy, which blasted holes through their armoured space suits. The more dead bodies hit the ground, the more Charlie got carried away using his cannons. But Charlie's health had dropped dramatically: his body display showed his energy was below 30 per cent. A.L.I.C.E. had been right. He was close to using up all his energy, and he found himself slumping to his knees.

'Charlie, your excessive use of the cannons is having a detrimental impact on your health,' A.L.I.C.E. warned.

His moment of weakness left Charlie taking a hit to the shoulder. It wasn't enough to knock him over, though, and soon he was back on his feet returning fire while he retreated to a disused shipping container close by. He collapsed to the ground, exhausted. There, he stared blankly at his body's health display. Two tiny vertical bars flashed a bold red: 20 per cent.

'Charlie, you must disengage your arm cannons at once!' exclaimed A.L.I.C.E.

'But I'm winning!' Charlie said, panting.

'If you continue, you will self-terminate.' A.L.I.C.E.'s words turned Charlie cold.

'But how can I stop them otherwise?' Charlie groaned. 'There's too many of them for me to fight single-handedly. I can't allow them to leave here. I can't put my town in danger.'

'There may be another way.' A.L.I.C.E. scanned the building's exterior. 'I have detected a weakness in the outer wall. If you aim precisely for the area above the third window up, you will cause the middle section of the building, where the aliens are exiting from, to collapse.'

'How sure are you?' Charlie asked.

'By my calculations, the chance of succeeding is 92 per cent,' replied A.L.I.C.E.

'That's good enough for me,' exclaimed Charlie.

Charlie sprang out from behind the metal container, took out seven or so aliens that were in close range, then fired two shots above the broken window on the third floor. Just as A.L.I.C.E. predicted, the wall collapsed like a pack of cards and crashed down on top of the aliens, killing all those below. The two dozen aliens that survived, Charlie finished off with efficiency, then carried out a scan of the vicinity.

'I am not picking up any signs of alien life form,' said A.L.I.C.E. Charlie drew a long breath of relief. He turned to face the night sky and saw to his surprise that the alien spaceship had disappeared.

'Where did it go?' he said.

In the distance, two little white lights became visible in the darkness. There was a dull chopping noise. The sound grew loud very quickly. Then a light aircraft came into view, taxiing away from them down the broken tarmac. Charlie detected two human heat signatures on board the plane. He was convinced one of those was Salvador, and he took aim at the aircraft. He was down to his last bar of energy.

'Charlie, I ask you to reconsider your actions,' A.L.I.C.E. implored.

'Why, because you want to protect Salvador? Is that it?' Charlie said, fuelled by anger towards the callous man.

'Because it would be morally wrong to consider harming another human being if you cannot confirm their identity,' said A.L.I.C.E.

Charlie gritted his teeth in silent fury, still aiming at his target. He ignored A.L.I.C.E.'s plea. She continued, 'Charlie, do not allow your emotions to overrule your good sense. You have a responsibility to protect mankind with these new powers you have obtained – do not seek to destroy it.'

At the last second, Charlie disengaged his arm cannons, lowering them to his side just as the front wheel of the light aircraft lifted from the tarmac. His health slowly started to return. Charlie looked on bitterly as the small plane took to the dark skies. He sighed, feeling guilty. 'You were right, A.L.I.C.E. I don't know what came over me. What was I thinking?'

'Power can easily corrupt the mind,' said A.L.I.C.E. 'You made the right decision, Charlie. Do not be too harsh on yourself.'

Once the sound of the aircraft had faded into the background, the airfield fell silent, as it had been when Charlie arrived earlier that evening. All that could be heard was the crackling of the flames dying out. Charlie looked down at his hands. They'd returned to their normal appearance, but were trembling and burning with pain.

'I can hardly bend my fingers,' Charlie said.

'There are limits to the use of your symbiotic power, Charlie. You must learn to stay within the boundaries. You need training,' said A.L.I.C.E.

'I hear you,' Charlie said.

While Charlie stood flexing his fingers, a sound caught his attention. Instinctively, he looked around. Dread gripped him. Standing on top of the mound of fallen bricks in the gaping hole Charlie's cannon had made in the building was a beefy figure.

It was the alien General.

CHAPTER 14

ONE SHALL STAND, ONE SHALL FALL

The General moved its head fractionally from side to side, as if it were taking note of all the dead bodies lying before it. That would not please the General, Charlie thought.

Once the General had finished scanning the areas, it tipped its head back and stared up at the night sky. Charlie thought it looked sad. Was that possible?

'Yep, that's right! Looks like your space buddies have left you stranded here all alone!' Charlie hollered, thumbing upwards. The General did not respond. Instead it continued to stare at the stars.

'Do you think it can understand me?' said Charlie.

'If it has the intellect to communicate verbally with humans, it is choosing to ignore you,' replied A.L.I.C.E.

'How rude.' Charlie tutted.

The General eventually lowered its head and pressed a button on its waist, releasing a small cylindrical device. At one end of the device, a tiny propeller unfolded. The General let go of the device, which whirled in the air. It didn't go far, remaining within arm's reach.

Charlie was curious. 'What's it doing?' he asked.

'It appears to be checking the air quality,' said A.L.I.C.E.

'What for?' Charlie said, baffled.

A few seconds later, three small lights on the cylinder turned red. The propellers ceased operating and the device fell back into the General's hand. He dropped it, then pressed a button on the side of its helmet. A small tube that connected the General's helmet and body amour disconnected. A jet of white gas spurted out.

'Is it doing what I think it's doing?' said Charlie.

'It would appear so,' A.L.I.C.E. said.

The General removed its helmet. Charlie saw the alien's face for the first time, and gasped.

The monstrous grey face of the alien bore no resemblance to a human face. It had no nose. Above its four black sloping eyes, which were set back on its bulbous, hairless head, were holes that opened and closed. Were they part of its respiratory system? Charlie wondered. It also had no ears. But what Charlie found most disturbing of all, so gruesome that he wanted to look away but couldn't, was its mouth. It had no lips, just teeth. Long, sharp, cross-threaded teeth – and a lot of them. Unlike a human's teeth, the alien's teeth were sideways. It was most disturbing, especially when the General screamed at Charlie, revealing the horrible inside of its mouth.

Charlie gulped.

The General tossed its helmet away, sending it bouncing and rolling down the bricks. But it didn't stop there. It removed all its protective armour and discarded that too. Once unclothed, it held up its mighty battle axe.

'The alien wants to engage in hand-to-hand combat with you, Charlie,' A.L.I.C.E. said.

'Yeah, I'm kind of getting that impression. Well, if it wants a fight, it's gonna get one.' He took up a fighting stance.

'Charles, I ought to point out that you have yet to carry out training in hand-to-hand combat. Perhaps you should reconsider engaging with the alien?' A.L.I.C.E. suggested.

'That ain't gonna happen. If there's one thing you should know about me, A.L.I.C.E., it's this: I never run away from a fight. I started this mess and I'm going to finish it. It ends here tonight!' responded Charlie.

'Indeed, I am coming to learn that about you,' said A.L.I.C.E. 'In which case, it would be best to arm yourself. Are you ready?'

'What do you suggest? Laser guns, cannons? Something I can take it out with really quick,' Charlie said.

'Your symbiotic energy level is below 55 per cent. It would be unwise to use such weapons,' A.L.I.C.E. reminded him.

'Oh,' said Charlie.

'I recommend using a sword and shield – this will have less impact on your health,' said A.L.I.C.E.

'A sword? But I've never swung a sword in my life!' Charlie grumbled.

'Nor had you fired a weapon of any kind until recently,' A.L.I.C.E. pointed out.

Charlie shrugged. 'True. Alright, if that's what you recommend. Robonik, morph to sword and shield.'

Charlie's forearms reconstructed at his command. On one forearm appeared a long blue glimmering blade, and on the other a blue shield. His confidence revived when he saw his weapons, then he looked up at the General.

The bright moon shone down on the General like a spotlight. The General stood there, ready to engage in battle. All around them, small fires continued to burn. Charlie felt like a gladiator, about to do battle in a Roman colosseum. All he needed was a cheering crowd.

The pair exchanged hateful stares. Charlie brought the shield to his chest and tapped the sword against it – not to display his bravery but to check the shield's robustness against the mighty axe the alien General was grasping.

'Any advice, A.L.I.C.E., before I go to war with this alien creature?' he asked in a nervous voice.

'What you lack in skill, Charles, you make up for in speed,' said A.L.I.C.E. 'Be sure to keep out of its way. Strike when possible and move swiftly.'

Charlie nodded. 'Strike and move,' he repeated to himself. 'Got it.'

'One other thing, Charlie...' said A.L.I.C.E.

'Go on...'

'If you are struck by its weapon, you will be susceptible to damage,' A.L.I.C.E. said in a calm voice.

'But I thought the Robonik suit was indestructible?'

'The nanotechnology used to create the Robonik suit is a combination of nitinol and dyanik – the strongest material known to exist on planet Earth. The purpose of the Robonik suit was to enhance human capabilities in combat while at the same time providing a protective layer. This has dramatically changed since you absorbed the Blue Star's energy, allowing the nanobots to enter your bloodstream. You no longer wear the Robonik suit. You *are* Robonik, Charlie – and therefore you are indestructible. However, you're dealing with an alien life form, and its weapon has been manufactured using the material that now lives in symbiosis with you.'

'And you're only telling me this now!' Charlie said, feeling nervous.

'I have only just been able to carry out a detailed analysis of its weaponry. Please accept my sincere apologies,' A.L.I.C.E. said quickly.

Charlie didn't have time to ask A.L.I.C.E. if there was anything else he should know, for the alien General was thundering towards Charlie like a steam locomotive. Once on level ground, the General leapt into the air and swung the axe down towards Charlie.

Charlie reacted without thinking, and covered his head with his shield. The axe struck the shield, sending a surge of plasma energy rippling around them. Charlie did well to absorb the impact of the powerful strike. However, the General immediately followed up with a combination attack. Charlie managed to deflect both hits, but the second was so powerful that it threw him across the yard and into the chain-link fence.

He'd barely stood up when a warning came from A.L.I.C.E. 'Prepare to defend yourself, Charlie. Here it comes again.'

In no time, the alien General was upon him, wielding its axe. Charlie twisted sideways to escape, leaving the General's blade to slice through the metal chain fence like a hot knife through butter.

The General roared.

Charlie backed away.

All around the yard the alien stalked Charlie, slashing at him relentlessly. No matter how many times Charlie blocked and dodged the alien's vicious attacks, he didn't manage to attack the General once.

'Doesn't this thing tire?' Charlie said, catching a breather.

'Charles, you must do more to counter-attack.'

'Can't you see I'm trying?' Charlie yelled. 'For such a huge creature, it moves darn quick. I can't get anywhere near it!'

'As you did when you power-leapt, draw upon your symbiotic energy and speed-burst. You did this automatically when you ran up the wall. And be sure to counter-attack with your sword,' A.L.I.C.E. advised him.

'Got it,' Charlie panted.

The alien General came forward, swinging its axe. Charlie evaded it by sliding underneath. In the split second the alien had its back turned, Charlie swung his sword and slashed down the alien's back, leaving a deep laceration. The General gave a high-pitched roar that resonated for miles around; it sent a shiver down Charlie's spine.

'Oops, I think I've made it even angrier,' Charlie said, taking a step back as the furious alien turned to face him.

'Attack while it's injured!' said A.L.I.C.E.

Charlie yelled as he charged at the General, swinging his sword. However, it was a pathetic swing by his standards as a baseball hitter. The General saw it coming and blocked Charlie's attack with its axe. It followed up with a heavy punch that sent Charlie's head spinning. The second he came round, the General hit him with a powerful underarm strike that saw Charlie soar high into the air. He landed with a terrible crunch. Winded and hurt, he lay on the ground, semi-conscious. His energy level was critically low. To keep him alive and repair the damage his organs had sustained, his symbiotic energy had to disengage from the sword and shield. He was no longer covered in protective armour. His strength ebbed away. He lay there, groaning in pain, his mouth bleeding. His body returned to its normal size. He could hear A.L.I.C.E. speaking to him, but her voice was distant.

The alien General kicked Charlie over onto his back like a hunter kicks a maimed animal. The creature's evil eyes sparkled in the moonlight. Charlie could have sworn the alien was grinning at him. He had been defeated.

Then, as if time had slowed, Charlie watched helplessly as the axe was raised. He closed his eyes and prayed that he would see his dad again.

Suddenly, a sharp crackling sound zipped through the air, followed by the dreadful noise of tearing flesh. When Charlie opened his eyes, he did not expect to be alive and all in one piece. When he saw that it was the General who was severely injured, it came as a big shock to him.

The General stood frozen, wielding the axe, a hole blown through its abdomen the size of Charlie's fist. Luminous orange blood poured down its legs and onto the ground. It was difficult to tell if it was in any kind of pain, for its hideous face didn't expression emotion like a human face. A second flash followed, sending the alien tumbling backwards and crashing to the ground.

Charlie hadn't the faintest idea who'd killed the alien. For all he knew, it could have been Salvador. Perhaps he wasn't on the plane after all? But he was too weak to get up and find out who he should thank, or even defend himself against. Instead, he lay there in pain, listening to what he thought was A.L.I.C.E.'s voice calling faintly to him. Then a deeper voice joined the first, and he realised it wasn't A.L.I.C.E. after all.

His best friends were by his side.

Bridget gasped. 'Oh, Charlie!' she said, cupping her hands to her mouth.

Whizzy knelt to listen to Charlie's chest. He turned to Bridget, looking sad. 'He's gone, Bridge.'

'Gone, my butt,' Charlie croaked.

'You're alive!' Bridget said, her eyes filling with tears. Whizzy too looked on the verge of shedding a tear.

'You sissies are not blubbering over me, are you?' Charlie said. 'Please tell me you're not.'

Whizzy gave a fake cough. 'Wow, it really is smoky round here, don't you think, Bridge?' he said, fanning his face.

'Oh yeah, for sure,' Bridget said, smirking.

Charlie smiled. 'Yeah, yeah. Give me a hand up, would you?'

Charlie groaned as they hoisted him onto his feet. He threw his arms around the pair of them and hugged them affectionately. 'Boy, am I glad you showed up when you did. That thing was kicking my butt.'

'Well, we couldn't let you have all the fun, could we, Whizzy?' said Bridget. Whizzy was marvelling over Charlie's suit, stroking it with a finger, when Bridget thumped him in the arm.

'Huh?' replied Whizzy. 'Yeah, Bridget was adamant we couldn't leave without you. Lucky for you she shot it when she did. Have to hand it to her. She kept us alive.'

'Thanks, Bridget, I owe you one,' Charlie said, squeezing her arm.

'Actually, I believe you owe me three, but who's counting?' Bridget said, smiling.

'Where did you learn to shoot like that, anyway?' asked Charlie.

'My dad taught me. He takes me hunting with him sometimes. Don't you remember me telling you that?'

The boys shook their heads.

'Typical.' Bridget rolled her eyes.

A crackling sound came from the alien as it drew its last breath. The three of them approached it cautiously. They gathered around the creature and stood for a long time staring at it in silence. The dying flames from a small fire close by brightened its face.

'Man, that's one ugly creature,' exclaimed Charlie, pulling a face.

'I think I'm going to be sick,' Bridget said, turning green.

'I have to say, this is one time I'm pleased I can't see properly,' said Whizzy happily.

Bridget tipped her head back to look up at the night sky. 'Wherever in the galaxy that Blue Star came from, it must be pretty valuable for those aliens to travel all the way here to get it.'

'Your friend makes a valid point, Charlie,' said A.L.I.C.E. in his mind. 'If the spaceship has returned to where it came from without the Blue Star, there is always the possibility that it may return someday.'

'If they do, we'll be ready for them, A.L.I.C.E,' Charlie answered aloud, then realised what he'd said and clapped his hand to his mouth. Bridget and Whizzy turned to Charlie, surprised looks on their faces.

'What did you just say?' Bridget said, her eyes widening.

Charlie flushed. 'Er, I meant, now the spaceship's gone...'

'No, no, the part about Alice,' said Bridget. 'You heard him say Alice, right Whizzy?'

'Wait a second!' Whizzy smiled. 'Are you speaking to Salvador's computer – A.L.I.C.E.?'

'I take it your friends do not know of our relationship yet, Charlie?' asked A.L.I.C.E. in Charlie's mind.

'No, they don't,' Charlie answered.

'Are you going to tell them?' asked A.L.I.C.E.

'Yes, when I'm ready to,' he thought to her.

'Perhaps you should—'

'Oh, would you be quiet and let me think?' Charlie said aloud. Bridget and Whizzy fell silent.

'Charles, the authorities have been alerted. You and your friends might want to consider vacating the area now.'

'Okay, A.L.I.C.E.,' replied Charlie aloud. 'Darn!'

'I knew it!' Whizzy said, dancing around in excitement. 'I thought I'd imagined it when I heard you talking to yourself before you broke through the outside wall. How is that even possible?'

'It's complicated,' said Charlie.

'You know she's, like, the smartest computer on the planet, right?' Whizzy commented.

'Oh, don't I know it,' said Charlie.

'And those things you fired at the spaceship – what was that all about?' Bridget joined in, but Charlie wasn't paying attention.

'I like your friends,' said A.L.I.C.E. through his mind.

'They can't hear you, so be quiet,' Charlie said irritably.

'She can hear me? That's crazy!' said Whizzy, who was hyperventilating in excitement. 'Ask her how far away the moon is from Earth—'

'Two hundred and thirty-eight thousand, eight hundred and fifty-five miles away approximately,' answered A.L.I.C.E. without hesitation in Charlie's head.

'No, no, on second thoughts that question's too easy, and I already know the answer. Ask her where the blue crystal came from,' Whizzy said.

'The Blue Star was taken from a planet in the Xia system by—'

'Just shut up for a second, both of you!' Charlie yelled.

'Apologies, Charles. I can see I am causing you emotional distress. I shall leave you in peace,' said A.L.I.C.E.

'Thank you,' replied Charlie in his mind.

'Sorry, mate,' said Whizzy.

'Look, there's a lot I don't understand about what's happened to me, and I'm still trying to come to terms with it. Having her – it – whatever this is inside my head,' Charlie said.

'She's in your head?' said Bridget.

'Yes, she's in my fricking brain!' Charlie said, jabbing his finger at his head. 'Look, we can discuss this later. We need to get out of here.'

'But what am I gonna say to my parents when I get back home? Where will I say I've been for the past two days? I can't exactly tell them about all of this. They'll think I'm crazy,' said Bridget.

'We'll figure something out on the way back,' said Charlie.

Seconds later, the children heard police sirens wailing in the distance.

'Let's get out of here!' Charlie said.

The children darted between the fires, climbed through the gap in the fence, and ran as fast as they could across the field, just as a police car came tearing down the track.

CHAPTER 15

REPERCUSSIONS

*One year later after the events
at Baverslocke Airfield*

At a packed-out Howard J. Lamade Stadium in August, Debby and her fiancé Evan sat side by side in the stand, waving giant foam hands excitedly in the air. Alongside them were two other families: Bridget's and Whizzy's. They'd made the trip from Cravins Creek to support Charlie and his team, who had reached the final of the baseball Little League World Series.

Charlie had played so well throughout the tournament that a buzz had grown around him. Kids were asking for his autograph and for selfies with him. He'd been interviewed by ABC and ESPN. Videos of him smashing the ball out of the park in games had racked up hundreds of thousands of views on a new internet channel, YouTube. Things couldn't have been better for him. Charlie had turned into a celebrity in the baseball world overnight, and he was enjoying every minute of it. Everyone knew his name. Even the sports commentators were rooting for him: they had nicknamed him Cali's Golden Hitter.

Baseball had taken up so much of Charlie's life over the past twelve months, with team practice and travelling to and from games. This kept his mind occupied, though at times memories of that awful night at Baverslocke Airfield crept in.

In the dugout, staring blankly through the chain fence, Charlie cast his mind back to that night. On their long walk home, the friends had been silent. They'd been in shock, unable to process what had happened. To break the ice, Charlie cracked a joke. The others laughed. And then they began to talk.

They all agreed that they never wanted to live through anything like that again. Charlie then talked about the Robonik suit and A.L.I.C.E. – he was keen to explain to his friends that he wasn't crazy, that he really did have AI inside his head, speaking to him.

The worst part of the conversation was listening to Bridget tell them how she had been bundled into a black van on her way home by Salvador's men and taken to an abandoned house near Cravins Creek. The men had been scary and threatening. Charlie felt utter shame. He could scarcely bring himself to look at her. One question that worried the children – apart from what they were going to tell their parents – was: what happened to Salvador and his henchmen? They had seen the light aircraft take off and assumed that the evil villain had escaped. But what about all his men?

As they drew nearer to home, they knew they had to discuss Bridget's disappearance. They knew they couldn't tell the truth about the aliens – sometimes the truth is too strange to comprehend – so they had to come up with a simple, yet convincing, explanation for Bridget's disappearance and how the boys had found her.

When they eventually arrived at Cravins Creek in the dead of night, a nervous-looking Bridget knocked at her front door. The two boys stood behind her, exchanging anxious looks.

Charlie looked as if he was wearing his normal clothes. But he wasn't. It was a disguise: a nifty trick he was able to carry out by ordering the suit to mutate its appearance. A.L.I.C.E. had told him he would be unable to take off the Robonik suit ever again; it would always be a part of him.

When the door eventually opened, Bridget's mom, Sarah, stood there. She welcomed her daughter with open arms and tears of joy. Her shrieks woke Bridget's dad Mike and Bridget's fifteen-year-old sister, Brittony, and they ran down the stairs. Once the family's initial shock had ebbed away, and the relief of having Bridget safe and well had filled their hearts, they asked what had happened to her.

In the splendid living room, Bridget painted a vivid picture. She told them how she'd taken a shortcut through the forest on her way home from Whizzy's that day. In the forest, she'd encountered a black bear. Although the animal posed no imminent threat to her – it was on lower ground – the sight of it was enough to panic Bridget and set her off running. Further along the path, she missed her footing and fell down an embankment between the trees, landing in a small, rocky gorge which she couldn't escape from. Bridget did such a good job that for a second even the boys were convinced it had really happened.

Charlie then spoke up on the boys' behalf. He said how upset they were by Bridget's disappearance. They'd felt compelled to go searching for her that evening, and by chance they had found her in the forest. Charlie didn't sound as convincing as Bridget, but their story satisfied the Gunnarssons, who were eternally grateful to the boys.

As the night drew on, the children began to yawn. Sarah suggested they called it a night. She said she'd phone Chief Causeway to let him know Bridget had arrived home safe and well, and to call off the search. Mike insisted he take the boys' home. Charlie, Bridget and Whizzy hugged and said their goodbyes, and the boys hopped into Mike's pickup truck.

Mike dropped Whizzy home first, then Charlie, explaining to their parents what had happened and how their sons were heroes. Both sets of parents were shocked to know that their sons had snuck out in the middle of the night, but were relieved to hear Bridget had returned home safely.

*

From then on, the three families became a lot closer. But to this day, they haven't found out what really happened to their children that night in Little Valley. The friends swore that they would never tell another soul, so long as they lived.

Chief Causeway visited the following day. He wasn't just there to see how they were but to show he was doing his job: closing the file on the missing child. After listening to their stories and asking a few questions, he left, satisfied. However, not everyone was convinced by what the children had said. Officer 'Goofball' Balecoomb, as Charlie still called him, was suspicious, and his suspicion grew out of an article he'd read in the local newspaper while he ate at Dolice's café in town.

Gossip quickly spread through Cravins Creek about Little Valley's alien invasion. All the newspapers and TV outlets reported sightings of UFOs all over Little Valley, and that people were being abducted by Martians. Of course, newspapers always made up such stories to sell more copies. Public interest only grew further when TV stations ran stories on Little Valley's police officer, Matthew Taunk, who had responded to calls about a disturbance at Baverslocke Airfield. He claimed to have seen dozens of dead aliens lying on the ground when he arrived. Seconds later, a spaceship had come along and beamed them all up. When questioned about Officer Taunk's claims, the Little Valley police department said they had found no substantial evidence and the officer had been placed on long-term sick leave. The matter was now in the hands of the FBI. The FBI had arrived and sealed off the airfield, refusing to comment. This led to more questions: why were the FBI there? What did they have to hide?

An old man named Willy Fishburrel from Little Valley had told the newspaper that, on the night in question, he had been driving along Little Valley Road towards Baverslocke Airfield. Not far from the airfield, he had seen three young children; one girl and two boys, one of whom was glowing luminous blue, run across the road in front of his car. They had all disappeared. Not long after, Willy said, he had seen a UFO hovering in the sky above Baverslocke Airfield. It had remained for a few seconds before vanishing into thin air.

This statement about the children made Officer Balecoomb curious. When he left the café, he bumped into Charlie and his friends, who were walking past.

'Well, looky 'ere!' Officer Balecoomb said in a condescending tone. 'You must be Bridget, right? Y'know, the last time I saw you boys, you were looking pretty teary. I'm glad to see those tears have dried now that you, little missy, are back home. Have a good day, kids.' He tipped his hat at them and walked off.

The children whispered among themselves, shook their heads and carried on up the street.

'Hey, kids!'

The children halted and looked around. Officer Balecoomb was walking back towards them, grinning slyly. He stopped before them, tapping the rolled-up newspaper in his hand and screwing his face up as if something was troubling him.

'Y'know, it occurred to me while I was eating a delicious breakfast in the café and reading the newspaper. Something about this case. Just. Doesn't. Add. Up. Look at this town, for instance. It's dead – nothing goes on round 'ere. Same goes for Little Valley. Yet in the last few days, more things have happened than both towns have seen in years. Now, call me cynical if you will, but I find it rather peculiar that a young girl from a well-do-to family goes missing the same day a plane crashes in the forest. Then by some miracle she shows up nearly two days later with her friends, who just happened to have found her. And on the same night, a building at Baverslocke Airfield is destroyed, and nobody knows who was responsible. It all seems rather coincidental, don't you agree?' Officer Balecoomb narrowed his eyes at them.

The children looked at each other and shrugged, their expressions blank.

'See, here's what I think,' he said, stepping closer in an intimidating manner. 'I don't believe all this bull about flying saucers an' alien crap, but what I do believe is that you three troublesome kids knew about the plane that crashed in the forest. I'd go so far as to say you had something to do with that building being destroyed. Now, you may have got lucky with whatever it was you did, and you've got away with it this time, but sooner or later your luck's gonna run out. And when it does, guess who's gonna be there waiting to arrest you? You go on now.' And off he strode.

Charlie had known all along that Officer Balecoomb didn't believe their story, but what could he do? He had no proof that the three of them were connected to the Little Valley incident

Whenever the incident was discussed, Officer Balecoomb tried to slip into the conversation the possibility of the kids being involved. When he did this, Stan threatened to ship him off to the city to work, warning Balecoomb to stop reading idiotic drivel in newspapers and to get on with his job.

As for Salvador, the children never heard from him or saw him again. Robert Frieman of Amspatrax Tech Corp. released a statement that said: 'It is with great sadness that we announce that Enoch Salvador, the pioneer of space travel and technological robotics, has tragically died while on holiday overseas. Our condolences go to his family and friends. I have been appointed the new Chief Executive of Amspatrax Tech Corp.'

Charlie didn't believe that Salvador was dead. Every time he heard Salvador's name on TV, he shuddered and changed channel. He believed the evil villain was out there and still alive. But he found some comfort in knowing that the FBI was also looking into his company.

It took a while for Charlie to adjust to his new abilities and responsibilities, but the biggest change he had to adapt to was living with someone inside his head, 24/7. At first it was an enormous burden. But once he had set boundaries, it became less intrusive and more tolerable. As the months rolled by, it felt as if A.L.I.C.E. had always been there and he'd never lived without her.

Whizzy had been right. A.L.I.C.E. truly was awesome. She was the most advanced artificial intelligence computer in the world, and now she was also an evolving consciousness connected to Charlie by symbiotic energy. Thanks to A.L.I.C.E.'s advice and mentoring, coupled with training programmes, reading and mediation, and his two best friends to keep him grounded, Charlie became far less hot-headed and more understanding and sympathetic. Of course, his new powers didn't stop him from getting up to mischief...

*

'You're up, Charlie,' boomed his coach from the dugout.

Charlie shook his head to clear it, then picked up his bat and walked out of the dugout. The crowd went wild when Charlie stepped onto the field and casually walked over to the batter's box. Nervous excitement fluttered in his stomach.

'How are you feeling, Charlie?' asked A.L.I.C.E.

'I feel good,' replied Charlie, communicating mentally with A.L.I.C.E. 'But you already know that.'

'I believe it is polite to ask. However, in light of your recent loss of consciousness, I urge you to seek medical attention as soon as possible. As you know, I have been unable to determine the cause,' said A.L.I.C.E., sounding concerned.

'I will, I promise,' declared Charlie. 'As soon as the tournament's over, I'll go and get checked out.'

He stepped up to the batter's box and leaned down to brush away the dust that covered his gold Nike cleats. They gleamed in the sunlight. It was a scorching day, with not a cloud visible in the blue sky. The sun beat down. Spectators had gathered beyond the outfield fence sat on a grassy knoll facing the stadium. Only the fans in the top tiers of the stands were lucky enough to enjoy shade. The umpire stood behind Charlie. The catcher, who was pouring with sweat, removed his head guard to wipe his dripping brow, then put it back on.

'Hey, whassup?' said the chubby catcher, sounding as if he knew Charlie.

Charlie wheeled around to the catcher, who he didn't recognise. He acknowledged him with a jerk of his head. 'Whasupp,' he said and went back to mentally preparing himself.

The teams were tied at 3-3. Charlie needed to make his bat count if they stood a chance of winning the game. Even though Charlie was a brilliant batter, there was one person who could stop him, who had done it before: the pitcher, James Swindle.

Charlie first encountered Swindle when he was nine. Charlie was playing for his local team in California and Swindle had recently joined an opposing team for a season. Charlie's team thought it'd be a walk in the park that day against a team they often beat. But that wasn't to be.

Many of Charlie's teammates were struck out by the fast-bowling kid, including Charlie. Charlie was livid. He knew he'd met his match, and flung away his bat in a fit of rage. He'd remembered the boy's name ever since. When Charlie heard that a pitcher nicknamed the Cannonball would be playing at the tournament, he knew who it would be. He prayed that their teams would meet so he could settle the score.

'So, you're Cali's Golden Hitter?' said the chatty catcher.

'So they say,' replied Charlie modestly, gently swinging his bat back and forth.

'That's a pretty cool name, I'll give you that,' said the catcher. 'You see my man up there? They call him the Cannonball.'

'I know who he is,' said Charlie, gripping his bat.

'Oh, so you also know that he holds the Little League World Series record for the fastest ball thrown? Ninety-one miles per hour! I mean, damn, not even my mom's car can go that fast!'

'Ninety-one miles per hour, you say?' Charlie asked, sounding surprised.

'Uh-huh.'

'Humph. Let's hope he doesn't throw me a slow one like that, or I'll be truly disappointed.' Charlie took up his position facing the pitcher's mound, ready to hit.

'Whatever,' muttered the catcher, crouching down behind Charlie. 'Time to go to work, Cannonball! I got one right here for you!'

Though he couldn't hear them, Charlie's family and friends were going crazy chanting his name. Then the crowd quietened.

Luke Regus, Charlie's teammate, was edging cautiously out of the hot corner of third, ready to make a run for home. Swindle was keeping a watchful eye on him before turning to exchange glares with Charlie.

Charlie held his bat ready, his face stern and determined. Swindle glanced at third base again before winding up and unleashing the baseball. The ball flew down the middle. Charlie swung, but his bat met fresh air. The ball landed safely in the catcher's glove.

'STRIKE ONE!' called the umpire, giving a hand signal.

Charlie huffed and took a step back to compose himself, while the catcher tossed the ball back to the smirking pitcher.

The noise in the stadium picked up again. 'C'MON, CHARLIE!' Bridget and Whizzy and the others yelled from the stands.

Charlie stepped forward, his bat at the ready, only to see Swindle make a surprise throw to the baseman on third, almost catching out Regus, who had to dive back. It was a close call, but Regus just managed to stay in the game. The baseman threw the ball back to the pitcher.

'Same as before, Cannonball! I got you!' yelled the catcher, signalling with his fingers between his legs to Swindle.

The cheering quietened. Charlie stood, waiting for the ball. Swindle nodded to the catcher, wound up to pitch the second ball, and slung it with all his might.

'STRIKE TWO!' yelled the umpire. Hearing the words infuriated Charlie more than missing the ball.

Charlie could sense history about to repeat itself. He backed away to take a deep breath and have a stern word with himself. Jeez, that boy's got an arm on him, he thought. He seems to favour fast balls – chances are, he'll toss me another one. I need to distract him from his game – and I've got an idea. His lip quirked.

Charlie stepped to the plate, positioned himself, then suddenly pointed behind Swindle to the outfield, beyond where people sat on the hill. He was signalling where he intended to hit Swindle's ball.

Swindle's sweaty face turned red. 'No one's ever called shot on me before,' he muttered. 'I'll show him.' The catcher shook his head in dismay, while Charlie's teammates went crazy shouting his name.

The crowd anxiously awaited the final pitch.

Swindle nodded to the catcher. The wait for the ball felt like forever to Charlie. He relaxed his grip on the bat; he could feel himself growing tense. This was it. His last chance to set the record straight between him and Swindle. Everything was riding on this last ball. He wanted to win so badly – not just for himself, but for his team, who had worked tirelessly to reach the finals. It had been a dream come true to be chosen to play in the Little League World Series, and to reach the finals was beyond awesome. All eyes were on him.

A blue electrical current moved across Charlie's eye as he stared at Swindle, who stood motionless on the pitcher's mound. Then the moment came. Swindle raised one leg so that his thigh was parallel to the ground, twisted his body as he turned to wind up, then pushed off with his back leg, allowing his weight to shift forward suddenly to gain power. He threw the ball.

The spinning ball travelled through the air towards the batter's box. Charlie swung. This time the baseball didn't find the catcher's glove. Instead, it struck Charlie's bat and soared over Swindle's head into the deep blue sky, and came down somewhere over the outfield fence.

The stadium erupted into cheers.

Everyone was on their feet, cheering for Charlie. He tossed his bat away and started to run. Charlie's teammates jumped around wildly in the dugout as they watched. They couldn't wait to run onto the field to greet their hero as he ran down the final stretch towards them. The opposing side looked dejected.

An indescribable exhilaration filled Charlie as he ran over the final base to complete his victory home run. His team picked Charlie up and tossed him in the air. Charlie had done it – he had won them the game! They were the new champions of the Little League World Series!

When Charlie's feet finally touched the ground again, he turned to wave at the cheering crowd. As he did, he spotted his family and friends in the stands. Debby's eyes filled with tears of joy. Bridget and Whizzy were beaming.

Then something happened that wiped the smiles off all their faces.

Slowly, a shadow drifted over the baseball field, darkening the stadium. The noisy crowd fell silent. They looked up at the enormous black object floating in the sky, blocking out the sun. At first, Charlie hadn't noticed the change in their expressions. His attention had been drawn to a mysterious figure standing a few rows up from his family and friends in the stands. Oddly, he wore a dark trench coat, completely unsuitable for the heat. Charlie couldn't make out the man's face, which was shadowed by his hood.

When a scream rose from the crowd, Charlie looked away from the mysterious figure. He looked at the crowd and followed their line of sight. To his utter horror, an enormous spaceship hung in the sky.

'Charlie...' A.L.I.C.E. began.

'I know,' he said in dismay. 'It's here for me.'

CHAPTER 16

UNFINISHED BUSINESS

Six months after the events
at Baverslocke Airfield

In a grimy laboratory, a man lay on an operating table.

The man was Enoch Salvador.

His right arm, which had been amputated below the elbow some time ago, was being replaced with an advanced cybernetic arm Salvador had invented. Salvador was awake during the procedure, grimacing in pain.

'How much longer?' he growled at the surgeon.

The Ukrainian surgeon peered at Salvador over the top of his glasses while he carried out the surgery. 'Much time,' he said in broken English, his voice muffled behind his mask. ''Tis Very complicated.'

Salvador stared at the dim light shining down on him and clenched his teeth. 'Morphine! I want morphine!' he demanded.

The surgeon signalled to a Chinese woman who stood nearby. She looked nervous, but came over and injected something into Salvador's arm. His eyes turned heavy and drowsy. From then, Salvador said nothing more, and the surgeon continued to work in silence. The room was cold, but it did not stop beads of sweat dripping down his forehead. After several gruelling hours, the surgeon finally finished the procedure. He leaned back on the operating stool, exhausted. He wiped his brow and pulled the mask from his mouth.

''Tis done,' he said, sounding relieved. He pressed a button which raised the operating table to bring Salvador to a sitting position. Salvador still looked drowsy, but he brought his arm up to inspect the surgeon's work. He moved and flexed his new mechanical fingers, watching the tendon rods slide back and forth in his cybernetic forearm.

'What do you think? 'Tis Good, yes?' said the surgeon, worried.

'Fetch me a mirror,' Salvador said abruptly.

The woman swiftly brought one to him. Salvador took it from her with his mechanical hand and brought it close to his face. He stared for a long time into it, with a look that suggested he did not recognise himself. There were dark circles under his eyes, he had grown a beard, which was long and unruly, and his head had been shaven. Salvador turned his head to one side and brought his hand up to touch a small scar.

The surgeon watched him and shifted in his chair anxiously. 'As you see, neurochip implant in your brain 'tis success. You have control over new arm.'

'Indeed,' replied Salvador.

'It feels like you never lost your arm in the first place.' The surgeon chuckled nervously.

Salvador lowered the mirror and stared frostily at the surgeon; the surgeon gulped.

'You have no idea,' Salvador said stonily.

The surgeon swallowed. 'You must give your body time to heal and adapt to your new arm. Do not lift anything heavy,' he advised timidly.

Salvador grabbed the wires attached to his chest and pulled them out. He swung his feet from the operating table down onto the stone-cold floor and stood up. He turned, grabbed the operating table with his cybernetic arm, and slowly started to lift it. The surgeon watched in horror as the table rose above his head.

'Incredible,' Salvador said, grinning wickedly. He released his grip and sent the table crashing back down to the floor.

'You there,' Salvador said to the cowering woman, 'fetch me my shirt!'

The woman scurried to do as she was told.

Salvador slipped it on and began to fasten the buttons. 'How long before the virus is ready?' he said, without turning his head to acknowledge the surgeon.

The surgeon looked hesitant. He tugged at his collar. 'They working on it now. Twelve to eighteen months, maybe,' he replied.

Salvador paused fastening the last button 'Have it ready in six,' Salvador demanded.

'Salvador, please – 'tis not possible without additional resources.'

'I will order my men to bring you what you need to speed up the process, and my assistant Errold, who will prove greatly beneficial to you, once I've found where he's hiding. In the meantime, I suggest you get to work on the virus. Time is ticking,' Salvador said, wheeling around and glaring menacingly at the man.

He walked over to a rusted surgical table where a prosthetic arm and a black trench coat lay. Salvador stared at his old prosthetic limb before picking it up with his cybernetic hand and squeezing it.

'That boy,' he said in a low, grumbling voice. 'He will pay dearly for interfering in my business and stealing Robonik and the Blue Star from me.' Salvador flung the limb at the woman, who flinched.

'Get rid of this, and make sure I never see it again.' He slipped on the trench coat and drew the hood up over his head. 'The next time we meet, Urik, I expect my virus to be ready,' he said sharply and exited the rundown building.

Outside, a black vehicle waited in the dark. Salvador opened the rear door and climbed in. The driver looked at Salvador in the rear-view mirror.

'Have your men located Errold yet, Ramus?' Salvador asked.

'Yes, boss,' replied Ramus.

'Good. Have him brought here immediately – he has much work to do,' said Salvador.

'Will do,' said Ramus. 'Where to now, boss?'

Salvador thought for a second. 'First, we need to pay a visit to the new CEO of Amspatrax, Mr Frieman. I need to ensure my affairs are still in order. I can't have those meddling directors thinking they can take over my business now that I've officially been declared dead.'

'What about the kid, boss?' asked Ramus. He watched Salvador hold up his cybernetic hand. His eyes widened.

'Yes ... Charles.' Salvador stared at his mechanical fingers. 'I have unfinished business with him.' He laughed evilly.

The vehicle's bright brake lights went off. It pulled away slowly down the beaten dirt track and drove off into the night.

ACKNOWLEDGEMENTS

I would like to express my sincere gratitude to the people who have helped assist in the edit, proofread, typesetting, illustration and design of the *Charlie Robonik* book: Jane Hammett, Inkceptstudio, and Alice V. You have been truly marvellous to work with and I look forward to working with you again in the future on book number two.

And a special thanks goes out to every one of you across the galaxy who have read and shown love to the *Charlie Robonik* book, without your incredible support it would have not been made possible.

Oh, and one last thing,
A.L.I.C.E says "Thank You" as well.

Printed in Great Britain
by Amazon